# Growing Up Under Hitler –
# I Was There

## By

## Ludwig Wilhelm Knapp

*To Rosemary*
*Best Wishes*

*Ludwig W. Knapp*

ISBN: 0-7596-9818-X (E-book)
ISBN: 0-7596-9819-8 (Paperback)
ISBN: 0-7596-9820-1 (Hardcover)

This book is printed on acid free paper.

1stBooks - rev. 06/28/02

In writing this book, I found it most essential to be as accurate as possible; any errors are completely unintentional and, as author, my responsibility to correct in later editions.

Correspondence should be addressed to:

Ludwig Knapp
P.O. Box 5594
Clark, N. J. 07066

# Preface

For many years I have been urged by friends and relatives to write about my early years in Germany and about my experiences during and after World War II.

I finally sat down and put it on paper so that my children and grandchildren can read about an unknown side of the history of World War II and about how I survived the challenges in my life at that time.

I'll always remember my stepmother, Charlotte Kelch, who came to an area that was totally unfamiliar, willing to take up the task of caring for two young children she had never seen before. She arrived in the darkest time of the war with no assurance that our father would survive and return to us.

When our father did return unharmed, after almost six years of war, we were elated. Now, I had a father, whom I could count on for advice. In retrospect, it was always good advice and I heeded it.

I want to thank my wife of 45 years, Doris, for all the hours of typing and retyping in preparation of the manuscript also her commentaries, advice and constant support.

Thanks to my daughter, Karen Cammarata for typing the final copy and doing it so well. Thanks to Larry Golden and Norman Woerner for their input; thanks also to Oberstudienrat Hans-George Hoetger, Muelheim, Germany who has encouraged me to consider a German Edition.

Last, but not least, many thanks to Shirley Horner, book consultant and editor, who gave me excellent advice on improving my story.

Part One of my story will describe, in many chapters, my German family, the early years of the conflict, my time in the Hitler Youth Camp, my apprenticeship at Bayer. It includes an account of the final defeat of Germany, surviving shortages and illness, and the eventual comeback of my hometown and of the country as a whole. Here too, I recall my years at the Bayer Plant as an electrician and—finally, most important of all—the arrival of an invitation to come to the USA.

Part Two of the book will cover the early history of my hometown, Dormagen. Also, I include stories of survival, at war's end, by my father, seven uncles, a cousin and a good friend and others, who all served in the German Armed Forces. I also speak about collaborators, the Waffen SS and the Foreign Legion, the loss of life during the war; and the reasons, as I see them, why World War 1 and World War II occurred; also, the German Jews as scapegoats.

Fifty years later, my return trip to the Hitler Youth Camp in East Germany and the positive results of that visit are described. Finally, my life in the USA end the book.

I hope you enjoy this true story.

# Table of Contents

# Part One

# My Life as a Hitler Youth and Beyond.

*Ludwig Wilhelm Knapp*

# Chapter 1

# My German Family

My father, Karl Knapp was born in Offenbach, the town that borders the Glan River in the Pfalz, a scenic but at that time economically depressed region. The settlers of this area were known as hard workers, and many would eventually leave their homes to seek a better life, even emigrating to America. One of the most prominent persons from this site is former German Chancellor Helmut Kohl.

My father was one of five; he had a sister and three brothers. He too would leave his hometown in search for work, having learned the bricklaying and masonry trades. In the later 1920's, he did find a better job in the Koeln area about a hundred miles away, which at that time was busy with the construction of power plants that, fueled by soft coal, made it possible to produce energy economically for an extensive area.

In 1926, at the age of twenty-one, my father applied for a U.S. Visa. His next step was to inquire about the conditions then existing in America. An aunt who had recently returned from the U.S. after her husband's death did not provide an encouraging picture. To his surprise, she discouraged him and thereby changed his mind. The result was that he gave the visa to Albert, his youngest brother who looked like him, but who, unlike my father, was unemployed. Thus Albert Knapp, who became Karl Knapp, crossed the big water to live happily ever after in the state of New Jersey until his death at the age of seventy-five. In turn, he helped his older brother, my Uncle Ludwig, come to America. The next year, Ludwig's wife, my Aunt Frieda, and their son, Herman, arrived. (Herman, Lt. Col. USAF was KIA '68, VietNam). Both uncles worked many years at the Procter & Gamble plant in Staten Island, New York.

My mother, Gertrud Paefgen, was born in 1908 in Dormagen. She was one of six children, three boys and three girls, all tall and slim, they were nick-named "the reeds". If they minded, it did not matter. Naturally my mother called my father "Schmal," meaning slim. Her parents owned and operated both a milk delivery

3

business and a small grocery store, and I can still remember my mother giving me raisins that were on sale in the store. Her mother, Josephine Paefgen, was also a skilled midwife who had helped many locals enter this world. Since my mother's parents died early, I do not remember them, but the milk and grocery business was continued by my mother and my Uncle Josef.

Since the milk business operated through the use of bicycles, it required workers with great physical stamina, who were friendly and patient. I can still see the heavy milk cans hanging on the handlebars of the bikes ridden by my mother and uncle. The delivery service went door-to-door, measuring out the milk into the customer's containers. This was before the days of individual containers.

Soon after my parents married in 1929 (they met locally at a dance in town) my father opened his own business in the back of our house. He produced and installed (both for new homes and for alterations), the following: steps and stairwells, window sills, floors and wall tiles. He also filled many cemetery work orders - gravestones and border stones - mostly making the pieces himself out of concrete and mixtures of terrazzo and art stone.

I was born on September 1, 1930, named after one of my father's brothers. Three years later, my sister, Else, was born in September 1933. I would like to note here that since my father was born on August 3, 1905, we did have an unusual distinction in common: World War 1 began in 1914 on my father's ninth birthday; World War II began in 1939 on my ninth birthday. When my son, Jeffrey, celebrated his ninth birthday, the U.S. was in the thick of the Vietnam War. (Will mankind ever learn to live in peace?)

To return to the years of my youth, it was a time when orders came in to my father on a regular basis, but payment for completed work left much to be desired. I recall my father telling me the following: Herr Schick, one friendly neighbor, ran a business that delivered large items from the local railroad station to the recipients who had ordered them. One day, Dad spotted a sturdy new bicycle in Herr Schick's wagon load and inquired to whom it was going. When Dad learned that the owner-to-be was a man who owed him large amounts of money, he gave the agreeable driver a receipt and removed the bike from the wagon for himself. One might say, "God helps those who help themselves!"

4

# Chapter 2

## Changes In 1935.

In 1935 a new school was built, a ten-minute walking distance from my home. This solid brick building, intended to serve grades 1 through 8, was named the Langemarck School in memory of a World War 1 Flanders Battlefield, an area where many young Germans had the "honor" to die for their Kaiser. I liked school and had good grades.

The new school, of course, would be decorated with the new Third Reich symbols. A sculpture about 15" x 28" in size and cast in sandstone, portrayed first a boy and then a girl in Hitler Youth uniform, flanking the letter "S" in the archaic runic form. If that image sounds mysterious to you, just picture half of the Waffen SS insignia.

The order from City Hall to install the three stones was given to my father. I remember them, before installation, they looked down on us when the Swastika flag was raised on national holidays. Indeed, their life span was as short as that of the Third Reich.

Coincidentally; in 1945 shortly after my Dad's return from the war, he received a request to remove these reminders of Adolf Hitler. The job required the erection of a 25-foot scaffold and careful slow hand chiseling of the three castings. This type of work was often reserved for known ex-Nazi party members. However at City Hall, someone knew this was not the type of job to be given to an inexperienced and unwilling person. For this reason my father was chosen. I can still see the grin on his face after completing the job. As it happened, the school at that time was serving as a home for British occupation forces of my hometown. Looking out their windows as he worked, the British soldiers concluded from the nature of the task that this contractor must be an ex-Nazi. With a big grin on their faces, they asked him "Nazi, huh?" My father grinned back and continued the job until completion. A man who had survived almost six years of war could also find humor in the situation, as did the British soldiers. The traces caused by removing these symbols can still be seen over fifty years later.

However, in 1936 the new school was opened and I entered first grade. A year later a new gym was added, soon to be followed by a new Hitler Youth home nearby. The Boy Scouts of Germany were disbanded by Hitler and incorporated in the new youth movement. Their new home gave these boys a new place to meet and undergo training sessions.

During my first school year, I was struck by diphtheria, a dangerous childhood disease at the time. After six weeks in a local hospital I overcame it and to the amazement of my mother, graduated from the first to the second grade despite the lost school time.

The year 1937 witnessed the crash of the Zeppelin Hindenburg in Lakehurst, N.J. with the loss of over ninety lives - it could have been more. I recall that the Germans blamed it all on the hydrogen-filled cells of the airship. The much safer helium was on the U.S. government's "Not for sale to Germany" list. Later, research revealed that other reasons might have caused the accident. What a painful loss it must have been to the Nazis to no longer possess the largest-of-its-kind airship flying under their new flag so majestically over many foreign lands.

The year 1938 brought Cristallnacht. After Hitler's takeover, a constant hate campaign against the Jewish population of Germany was fostered by the government. We had about ten Jewish families living in my hometown. They lived in Dormagen for many years and were mostly small business owners who had a good relationship with the other townspeople.

One of my mother's close neighborhood girlfriends was Julchen W. and she was Jewish. I recall being in their home with my mother as a small boy. I also recall her crying to my mother complaining about the slowly ever-increasing pressure from the Nazis.

This all came to a blow-up in 1938 caused by an unusual incident. The German Ambassador to France, Ernest von Rath, was by all accounts, sympathetic to the plight of the German Jews, helping them with visas. A mentally sick Jewish man in Paris killed him, thus making a bad situation much worse. It set off Cristallnacht. All over Germany many synagogues and Jewish-owned businesses were destroyed or vandalized.

From the local scene I recall the following: A bright sunny day, the word among a group of youngsters was "let us go to the Nettergasse, a local street, there is something going on." When I got there, I saw a home being vandalized by a large number of kids, mostly preteens. (I was eight years old). I picked up a pot and ladle off the floor, made some noise by beating one against the other. Then I heard the word "POLICE." Dropping the pot and the ladle, I ran off, and looking back I saw how members of the local police force were driving the kids into the large garage and locking them there for a while - to scare them and cool them off.

When the local brown shirts leader, Herr D. received orders to destroy the town's Jewish stores and homes, his heart was not in it, and he let his reluctance be known. He looked at them as townspeople. But the Nazi leadership must have been prepared for this reaction. Their remedy: Send a brown shirt group from a larger, remote city to do the nasty job.

After Cristallnacht, it became clear to many Jewish people that remaining in Germany meant increasing danger. As a result, those who were able, left the country. The sad fact was: Many European countries and the USA showed great reluctance to receive refugees from Germany. At war's outbreak in 1939, Germany had 150,000 Jewish inhabitants remaining. The disappearance of my mother's close friend, Julchen, at this time, depressed her greatly because they had been good friends for many, many years.

*Ludwig Wilhelm Knapp*

# Chapter 3

# My Family's Fortunes: Reflections on the Ride to Hell.

As soon as they were married, my parents strived together to build a home. The chosen site was next door to their first home, and was actually the previous location of my grandparents' home now demolished and cleared away. The new solid brick building had three floors: The upper two floors for tenants and the ground floor for the Knapps. Although my father did some of the work, the bulk of the construction was done by contractors. To finance the project my parents, besides their savings, required a 10,000 RM (Reichsmark) mortgage. We did not know it at the time, but the ten-year loan would be paid with dubious war money and thus would not be paid off until 1948 when the hard-money reform was introduced.

During the construction period there were frequent delays, caused by material shortages. The reason: Germany was building its western fortifications, otherwise known as the west wall. That national undertaking swallowed large amounts of cement, lumber and steel. Luckily, our home was completed in 1939 shortly before the big bang!

During my school vacations from 1937 - 1939, my parents sent me by train to my grandmother's home in Elzweiler in the Pfalz. The little village was surrounded by hills; it had about fifty homes and a population of 280. The only major employment open to the males of the area was work in a stone quarry. There was little agriculture since the hills made cultivation difficult.

A group of friendly boys in this town my age made me welcome during the six weeks of vacation. There was no movie house or any other recreational outlets. There was a little stream forming the town's border. It was lined with trees and the stream in most places was less than a foot deep and only four or five foot wide. In between the tree roots and the rocks, trout managed to flourish. The local boys were quite skillful at catching the trout with their bare hands by searching under rocks and roots. Most fish were released, nobody bragged much about their skills, since fishing in the stream was illegal. However, the game warden never enforced the law.

Our main activity however centered around our attempts to destroy wasp and hornet nests. There were many to be found in the village or surrounding hills. Once a nest was spotted, the boys moved into position circling the nest. From a safe distance the following weapons were brought into play - stones, sticks, water, fire or sulfur sticks. Wasp and hornets were wild bees and considered a nuisance in contrast to honeybees which were useful and left alone to do their work. By the way, a hornet's sting can be fatal. We received many wasp stings while running away - fortunately never a hornet's sting. Since the country was hilly, we rarely tried to play ball.

One year when my father picked me up from my vacation - it was probably 1938 - he visited the bunkers that were under construction to be part of the west wall. The construction site was located at the next village, Welchweiler, on top of a hill. Many people who lived nearby were curious enough to come and look at the excavation and forms of the bunker to be prepared for concrete pouring. My father's curiosity about the details drew the attention of two plain clothesmen who must have been guards, judging by what followed. They approached him and questioned him closely. They knew that he did not live in the area. They possibly suspected that he was one of the American Knapps who had left the Fatherland for greener pastures. He eventually convinced them that although he had left his home area, he was now still living in Germany, the Koeln area. So much for my father, the spy.

We did not know it, but 1938 was to be our last summer at peace. When school vacation 1939 approached, I was looking forward to meeting my friends again. Staying at the grandmother's was not all playtime however. My grandmother, Aunt Emma and I spent many hours gathering berries or firewood in the nearby forest.

The game of "chicken" that Adolf Hitler had so successfully practiced since 1933 was coming to an end. The Polish situation was heating up rapidly - daily radio reports left little doubt about battles to come. We now had a new pastime: Visit a unit of

10

soldiers who manned a anti-aircraft battery on a nearby hill. We admired the equipment and enjoyed talking to the soldiers.

At the end of August my grandmother received a card from my Dad informing her that he had been drafted. War had not been declared yet, but he had the "honor" to be one of the first draftees for the war machine.

The west wall fortifications and their completion became top priority. For this purpose, the organization Todt was created - it was the equivalent of the American Seabees. They were given the job of completing the border fortifications. They wore khaki uniforms and carried no arms. Dad's postcard informed us that he was stationed near the Louxemburg border. Since he worked in the construction trade at home, he fit the bill for what was needed in the war effort. In this case, it was bad to be in the construction business, but in the long run it assured my father that he was not in the first line of fire during the many years to come.

My dad's sudden departure had a serious impact on my mother's mental condition (depression). She was now left alone with two young children and deep in debt for paying off the house. The Third Reich had no support groups or available psychiatrist to help instances like this. It was either do or die; sadly, in my mother's case it would be the latter.

I recall a car with a familiar license plate arriving in Elzweiler on that fateful Sunday. Any car coming into town caused attention, especially on Sunday. My mother had asked one of our neighbors and a close friend of my father's to take her to Elzweiler for the purpose of picking me up without delay. Herr P. Paas sure had a long drive that day to get us all home.

On September 1, all diplomatic exchanges were terminated, and German troops crossed the border into Poland. In spite of their speedy conquest, many of our military leaders knew that when France and England entered the war, the going would get tougher. The awareness of the possibility of a later U.S. involvement seemed to promise defeat since many of our leaders felt that history was going to repeat for those who refused to learn from it. But these men had entrusted their military oath to Adolf Hitler and the ride to hell had already begun and they were on board the bus!

*Ludwig Wilhelm Knapp*

# Chapter 4

# Germany at War: Tragedy for my Family

Propaganda is essential to insure the success of war. We had a master to lead that department. His name, Dr. Joseph Goebbels, who carried the title Reichs Propaganda Minister. He developed and sold the people on the following idea: If every household would have a "one pot" meal on one Sunday every month, the money saved could be collected and used for social services. The idea caught on and in the prewar years we had many "one pot Sundays." There was even a song dedicated to the idea in a satirical way; some of the words were: "And the little Joe runs through the hall, offering peas, beans, lentils - who wants seconds?" Since the Minister of Propaganda was small in stature, he was often referred to as "The Little Joe." Whether the funds collected were actually spent for social purposes is anyone's guess.

Another one of Goebbels' master strokes was the introduction of campaign songs. Whenever during the first half of the war, the German Army started a new campaign, it was announced in a special radio news flash. That news was followed by a special military song referring to the country that was then under attack. It was meant to raise the fighting morale of the Army and the homefront. The songs became very popular, but after Adolph Hitler uttered the impulsive declaration of war against the U.S., our propaganda master changed his tunes. The aggressive songs became more realistic. They did not have the same effect any more. Why? - because after 1943 the war had turned against Germany. We did not have much to crow about anymore. The Propaganda Minister ended his and his family's lives by taking poison in the last days of the war.

The Polish campaign lasted three weeks and ended in September 1939. The Blitzkrieg had turned into a Sitzkrieg (sitting around) along the western front. French and German forces sat in their fortifications; hostilities were confined to nightly scouting patrols.

13

The war on the high seas continued. The British Royal Navy were trying to keep the sea lines open, while the German submarines were trying to close them.

As the first Christmas of the war years approached, our mother's health grew worse. My father was given a "doctor's requested leave" and came home for the holidays. The hoped-for Christmas with the entire family present, however, was not to be. On December 17, 1939, while our father accompanied my sister and me to school to see a Christmas play, our mother committed suicide. She must have sensed that the war to come would bring a great sorrow to the world. The loss of our mother was extremely painful to all of us, but the ongoing war took our minds off that sad fact - most of the time.

After Christmas my father returned to duty with his unit. His unit of builders was to be turned into regular soldiers. They were stationed at Detmold in Westphalia.

My sister, Else, was now going to live with our second-floor tenants, Herr and Frau M. Schwidden, a childless couple. My sister was six years old, and they took good care of her. I was nine years old and went to live next door at my Uncle Josef's and Aunt Minni's home. She had just given birth to her first child, our cousin, Franz Josef, named after our late grandfather.

My uncle carried on with the milk delivery business without my mother's help, but was assisted by his wife part-time. Obligations of motherhood came first.

The Koeln area of the Rhineland was mostly Catholic. So, with the age of ten approaching, I prepared to take my first communion in our hometown church. The other communicants were mostly from my school class.

In May 1940 the German Army started a blitz attack on our western neighbors. It mattered little that three of the four nations attacked were not even in a state of war with us.

France was the target but this time a repetition of World War 1 trench warfare did not figure in the attack plan. It turned out that the Allied Forces of 1940 were no match for the force and strategy of the German Army. For both sides, the numbers in men and equipment were about even. Our early air superiority decided the fate of the Allied Forces and France. Four years later the roles would be reversed. The Germans would be the hunted.

14

My father's army training was completed in May 1940. Before his unit joined the western campaign he met the woman who would be our future mother. Her name was Charlotte Kelch. She lived near Herford and worked in that city for the railroad. After his move to France they stayed in touch by mail.

His new branch of service was to be in the construction engineers. That outfit's first assignment: repair roads and airfields. The airfields were to be used in the upcoming air campaign against England, a confrontation also known as "The Battle of Britain".

In the fall of 1940 my father attended and graduated from N.C.O. School. He was now a corporal and kept that rank for five years - odd? Yes! But there was a reason for it. According to my father's logic, any additional training that the army gave you kept you out of the frontline during the duration of that training and last, but not least, it raised your chances of survival. When, two years later, during the Russian campaign he was offered the opportunity to attend officer's school he turned it down. The situation had changed. Germany was then at the peak of its power and seemed invincible. In my father's mind, this meant German occupation to be in force over many countries. He did not want to be a part of such an expansion, possibly in the role of officer and having to remain in service. His conclusions - lay low and you might get out. He did a lot of long- range planning and was seldom wrong.

Back at the home front the air attacks by both sides were increasing in number and ferocity. Civilian casualties began to mount, especially in England, since German plans called for the destruction of many targets in preparation for an invasion. Owing to luck and to the bravery of the RAF pilots, the Germans suffered heavy casualties and their plans changed. The invasion of England was postponed.

Adolf Hitler had always stated that the archenemy was communism, meaning the Soviet Union. Josef Stalin, Russia's leader, had kept his word toward Germany as expressed in their 1939 Pacts. The Russian trade supply was a reliable source of raw material for the German war machine. However, the German people were told: "We need more living space for our people, let's take it in the east. Besides that, Russia is ready to attack us anyway." Later reports found this to be untrue.

# Chapter 5

# KLV CAMP

Late in 1940, for the sake of safety, the British government started to send children from southern Britain to more northern areas or to Canada. The intention was to remove them from the bombing and to place them with foster parents. Germany had a similar program. Parents could participate in KLV, which stood for Children's Land Evacuation. Children from 10-14 years old were given a chance to go from the western part of the country to the east. The bombers at that time had a shorter range of operation than they have now. For that reason, the north of England and the east of Germany were safe and could promise undisturbed sleep for the youngsters.

There was one major difference between the countries - England relied on foster parents to supply a homelike atmosphere. Germany saw an opportunity to start early training and indoctrination of the 10-14 year old boys. Where foster parents were used for the girls, camps of twenty-five provided shelter for the boys.

My father, now in France, wrote to us regularly. The army life seemed to agree with him. Some of the pictures reveal that he had gained weight. His uniform was quite stretched. In contrast, some years later, the strains of the Russian campaign showed on his photos. His uniform and his suits look far too big due to the obvious weight loss. One could judge by the later pictures how the fortune of war had turned.

Also, my father, who had written regularly to his ladyfriend, probably in 1940, decided that she might be our new mother. During his next army leave, January 1941, he introduced her to my sister and me. We were favorably impressed and hoped for the best.

The same month, January 1941, six of my school classmates and I were notified that the train would take us to the KLV Camp. The date was January 26, 1941, destination Lengefeld in the Ore Mountains, close to the Sudeten land border. Since my father was still on leave, he took me to the railroad station. The train was

17

very long and must have transported closed to 1,000 boys to the East.

Our camp was to be located in a large two-year old schoolhouse. Several of the rooms were reserved only for our use. Two large rooms served as day, and all-purpose room and classroom. A separate room served as sleeping quarters. The camp leader and the team leader had their quarters on the second floor above us. We also had the use of a large gym.

The food was prepared by the school's custodian couple, Herr and Frau Lerchner. It was brought from the nearby kitchen to our dayroom which served also as dining room. The chores of setting tables and serving food were performed by our kitchen service - two boys. Two other boys were responsible for house cleaning. The chores were rotated among us. Heinz B., one of my hometown friends, and I were assigned the daily mail pickup in town. It was a fifteen-minute walk to the town's center where the post office was located. Thus, we were exempted from the daily household chores.

Our team consisted of twenty-five boys, eleven-twelve years old, mostly from the city of Neuss and its vicinity; the second largest group was from my hometown, Dormagen. Since at age ten I was the youngest member of the crew, I did not yet belong to the Jungvolk, the junior group of the Hitler Jugend. That was soon to be changed. My age did not exempt me from the team leader's wrath, and I was frequently slapped for not being fast enough. The team leader, who was sixteen-seventeen years old, was himself a leader in the senior group of the Hitler Youth. Each leader in the senior group had volunteered for a six-month period and would later be replaced by a new youth. These leaders were the products of the national society, and we were to be molded after them. By war's end, most of them had paid for their enthusiasm with their lives.

One of the boys from Neuss had come from an orphanage. He was a husky, friendly boy. His name was Josef Pasternak. When it came to self-sufficiency; he was our teacher. He showed us how to press the uniform pants so as to leave a sharp crease and how to darn our socks. There is an art to weaving to close a hole.

Our afternoons were taken up by sports, swimming, marching, learning songs and other training, all under the watchful eyes of the teamleader.

The food, and the amount that was served to us, was rationed, just as was happening in the rest of the country. Bottom line - the food was nothing to brag about. However, one unusual fact - in twenty-seven months of camplife our group had no need for a medical doctor. We had plenty of fresh air and exercise and our minds were kept busy. Cuts and bruises were tended to by the campleader.

Once a year there was a sports contest. All members of the Jung Volk participated. To be declared a winner you had to accumulate 180 points. The contest consisted of three categories: 60 meter run, broad jump and distance throwing of a soft ball. All winners received a Victory pin - that covered most of us.

Our sleeping quarters consisted of bunkbeds. No fancy mattress, just a straw-filled bag with sheets and blankets and a pillow. A small locker for our underwear was kept near our bunks. There were daily inspections of the lockers and bunkbeds. Everything had to be folded in a certain way. The first few months, washing yourself and brushing your teeth was also subject to inspections. After we had developed the desired habits, the inspections were reduced.

Now let me introduce you to the camp leader, Herr Heinrich Steffens, fifty years old, a grade school teacher who had taught in Neuss. Since he was a teacher, he was also a Nazi party member. By the end of 1940 he was given a choice - To contribute a little more to the war effort, he could become a French POW camp commander or take charge of a KLV camp consisting of 25 boys and continue teaching grade school. He chose the latter.

Even today it is hard for me to imagine a teacher who could have been more enthused about our leader Adolf Hitler than Heinrich Steffens. Every school day began with a morning formation and a ten-minute talk about our leader, Adolf Hitler. On Sundays we received a double-dose of Adolf administered by Heinrich. He made every effort possible to replace our God with Adolf Hitler - not only on Sundays.

On Hitler's birthday, April 20, 1941, I was inducted by our camp leader into the DJ, the junior organization of the Hitler

Youth. Heinrich must have felt good about that, since his entire band would now wear a brown shirt. The last black sheep, myself, was now "incorporated." Most of my friends had uniforms which they wore proudly. Looking at an old picture, I see that I am wearing a First Communion suit. Well, I was a little over ten years old and did not know the meaning of "politically correct."

In all fairness, Heinrich never picked on me, possibly because my father was already serving in the army so early in the war.

# Chapter 6

# Reversals

The first eighteen months of the war saw our submarines inflicting heavy damages on the British Merchant and Naval Fleet. This was about to change. By the use of sonar, the British succeeded at sinking our major submarines. Germany saw three of its leading killer subs sunk within two months.

My dad's unit was now transferred east to Poland near the Russian border. It became apparent that the bitter lesson learned by Napoleon in 1812 was lost on our leadership. Adolf Hitler believed in his own invincibility, just like Bonaparte. Germany's initial success in June 1941 in the attack against the Soviet Union inspired high hopes for a speedy ending. Failure can be attributed to the harsh treatment inflicted on the Russian POW's and on the population in the occupied areas by the conquerors. Many Russians did not like communism and thought of the Germans as liberators - even greeting them with flowers. The hopes of the Russian people were soon dashed. There is a saying in Russian: "If you get bitten by a dog, it may as well be your own, instead of a strange dog."

We were told by our leadership that the Russians are subhuman and we should treat them as such. Nobody pointed out that the European part of Russia was developed by the Vikings and its Asian part by Ghengis Khan's descendants, who would prove to be a match for any foreign intruder. It did not take long for the once-sympathetic Russians to turn into fierce fighting partisans who contributed greatly to the eventual defeat of the German invaders. Today, almost sixty years later, I still think about the subhuman ideology of our leaders when I watch sports events that involve Russian athletes. They certainly look a lot more "Aryan" than did our leaders. So much so that when we invaded the Soviet Union, the world, watching the advance of the invaders, was amazed to observe that the German troops, like Napoleon's Grand Army, also included many other nationals who had decided - willingly or otherwise - to follow Hitler.

21

At our KLV camp we listened and cheered at the radio reports - little did we know.

My father's letters came from the center of the Soviet Union. His unit was involved in the construction of roads and bridges, and I received his letters on a regular basis. When we picked up our camp's mail at the town post office, we also received the daily papers. I recall the Pearl Harbor attack headlines. Two days later in December 1941, Germany declared war on the USA, thereby sealing its fate. It is correct to say that there was friction between the Western allies, but those differences were small in comparison to the difficulties that prevailed among the Axis powers. The three Axis countries were united by name only; each member acted for his own national interest.

There was no agreement about priority as existed among the western allies.

The 1941/42 winter in Europe was one of the coldest on record. Since Germany had hoped to finish its Eastern campaign before the onset of cold weather, its forces were ill-prepared to face the brutal cold. The Russians counterattacked and regained some territory. An appeal by the German leadership urged that all Germans contribute warm clothing and skis for the troops in Russia. There was a good response. Nonetheless, the effects of the cold weather was felt much more by our troops than by the Russians, who were better equipped with winter clothing and already possessed equipment that would withstand low temperatures. This inequity caused the first reverses on the battlefield, but a major front breakthrough was prevented by the bravery of the German soldiers at the high cost of their lives.

After a youngster stayed six months in the KLV Camp, his parents were given a chance to express their wishes, whether to have their son return home to the air-raid areas or to permit him to stay for another six months. Our campleader convinced all of us to stay for another six months and asked our parents to vote accordingly. As a result, we all stayed a full year. Since, in my own case, I did not have a home to return to, I had the "honor" of receiving a total of 27 months of the finest National Socialistic Indoctrination administered by Heinrich Steffens. If he had known that shortly after my camp departure, I would be attending my home church again, he would have classified me as a complete failure.

When, in the spring of 1942, the ground on the Eastern Front had dried out sufficiently, the German Army was on the advance once again. Deeper into Russia - or deeper into the meat grinder?

In the summer of 1942, our camp leader Steffens took a month's vacation and returned to Neuss, his hometown, and to his family. He had a unique family. His three daughters all held offices in the BDM (Bund Deutscher Maedel) the female branch of the Hitler Youth. They must have tried very hard to please their father. All of them married Waffen SS Officers. Their father was very proud of them. As a result, he often told us stories about events, ending them with the statement - "I know this from a reliable source" referring to his sons-in-laws.

I had an opportunity in 1942 to see my father when he was home on leave and suffered an allergic reaction landing him in Augustinus Krankenhaus, a hospital in Dormagen. My aunt urged me to also use this visit to pay respects to the priest of our church, Pastor Dresbach. When he opened the door, he was quite surprised to see one of his flock, now dressed in a brown shirt and saying, "Heil Hitler, Herr Pastor." You can perceive his sentiments when I tell you I had little chance to talk before he closed the door. (It is worthwhile to note that in 1943 when I was finished with the KLV camp and started attending church services, that this same pastor approached the pew where I sat and seeing that I was dressed in regular garb, whispered, "I am happy to see you. For a while I thought I had lost you," thus revealing his sentiments.

During our camp leader Steffens absence he was replaced by a local teacher, who was a more down-to-earth guy. The new leader took us on field trips showing us defense churches - there was a number of them in the border area. They had offered protection to the local townspeople during the raids of roving bands. These historic raids occurred during the many religious wars that the area experienced over a period of hundreds of years. The walls of these churches were of very thick stone construction so that no evidence of wood was visible.

The field trips took us through woods and fields littered heavily by cow droppings. Our leader explained to us that these droppings, once dried over the winter, made an excellent herbal tea. As part of our daily fare, we were mostly served tea. As a result of our field trip education, whenever our tea did not taste just right, we classified it as "cow shit tea again." Could this have been the reason why we stayed so healthy and did not need a physician?

## Chapter 7

## Defeat

With the arrival of winter 1942/43, advances on the Eastern Front slowed down and reversals occurred. The German Army faced a do-or-die battle at Stalingrad. After their loss at Stalingrad, the Russian Army went on the offensive for the remainder of the war. Goebbels, our Minister of Propaganda, declared at a big N.S. party meeting, that we are "now conducting total WAR and our enemies should beware!" I believe that at this point many Germans felt that the war would eventually be lost by Germany. However, any talk to that effect was judged as an act of treason and dealt with accordingly.

On January 30, 1943, Adolf Hitler had, for ten years, controlled the helm of Germany. No doubt those were the most turbulent years in the country's history, the worst was yet to come.

On that evening of the tenth anniversary I received the beating of my life administered by the camp leader. It happened the following way: It was supper time and we were eating. One spot at our table was empty because Karl Lamberts one of the campers, was on milk detail. He and another guy had gone to town to fetch milk for the next day. During the war years, we ate many soups that sometimes defied identification. That evening was somewhat unusual because we were serving two half-portions of soups. One was sweet and tasted like pudding; the other was a ground pea soup. Now comes the problem-we had no extra soup bowl in which to save the second half for Karl. Jokingly, I suggested that we combine both portions into one bowl. Guenter Richards, who was ladling out soup, dared me to do that. Well. I did not want to back down on a dare so I filled the "mixture" into one bowl. Shortly afterward, Karl returned from town, sat at the table and tasted his soup mixture. After being informed of the details that preceded his return, he reported me to the camp leader who called me to his table in front of everybody and gave me a severe beating on my butt, using a furring strip. I screamed, but to no avail. Thinking back maybe the camp leader did not like the radio report from the Eastern Front and thereby found an outlet for his frustration.

Next day, Karl told me, "Had I known what the old man would do to you, I would not have reported you." That helped me get over my pain. All that punishment for the lack of an extra soup bowl. Yes, we had all kinds of shortages, but we were never short of instant discipline!

When the air raids in the Rhineland increased in severity, my sister, now ten years old, opted for KLV as well. She was sent to foster parents near Wuerzburg in the southern part of Germany. There was no indoctrination for her.

At the start of the program some trainloads of boys went to Switzerland, Germany's southern neighbor. Two weeks later they returned and went to camps in southern Germany. Was two weeks enough to convince the Swiss authorities that this was not a good business after all? The thought of their own youth catching the Nazi virus must have had a sobering effect on them. The money that the Swiss may have received however was another matter; it was always welcome until the end of the war. No questions asked.

# Chapter 8

# Family Reunion

Early in 1943 my father and his ladyfriend, Charlotte, decided to get married and not to wait until the end of the war. They wanted to provide a home again for my sister and me.

Our mother-to-be was twenty-five years old, my sister nine and I thirteen years of age. The young mother-to-be undertook a great responsibility to enter so uncertain a dark future, but she handled it very well. Accordingly, at the next vote at my KLV camp, my father voted to end my term. Our return trip home, to the air raid area, for better or worse, took place in May 1943. I was looking forward to our new life as a family. My mother-to-be picked me up at the Duesseldorf train station after the long train ride across Germany. We continued to our hometown Dormagen, only a short distance away. My sister joined us a week later. We were now a family again - well almost. Our mother-to-be and our father were not married yet. But have no fear, that would soon be corrected. Our German leadership had "invented" long distance marriage. The procedure went as follows: Dad went to his company headquarters at 12 AM June 1, 1943 somewhere in Russia - there he gave his marriage vows in front of the company commander. At the same time, our mother-to-be, gave her marriage vows to the Justice of the Peace at the City Hall in Dormagen. They were now legally married! A church marriage could be conducted at a later date. Many couples were united during the war years by this ersatz wedding. After all, the war took priority and required unusual procedures. We now felt like a family again, of course, even without the father. By 1943 there were many fractured families due to the army's manpower demands.

My sister and I attended our hometown school once again. All the former KLV camp boys were back in the same school class, except one, Helmut L. He came from a divorced family, and the camp seemed a better solution in his case. His prolonged presence at the camp, however, would soon put me into a dangerous position.

Several weeks after my return from camp, I received a letter from our camp leader. In it he informed me that he had recovered a flare pistol from Helmut L. When asked about it, Helmut stated that Willi and Ludwig had each a flare pistol. His, according to Helmut, was given to him by Willi and that I might have taken my pistol home with me. This was true. When Willi L. and myself were asked to check on dirty bedding which was stored in the attic some months before, we made a discovery. We found an open civil defense box which contained, among other items, two flare pistols. We could not withstand the lure of the pistols even if no ammunition was available. Result: Each of us took a pistol. Unknown to me, my friend, Willi L. had given his pistol to Helmut L. shortly before our return home. Since our camp leader was responsible for the contents of the civil defense box, he contacted me. In his letter he stated that unless the pistol was returned to him (he happened to be on leave visiting his wife), he would turn the matter over to the Gestapo.

I got the next train to Neuss, his home town, with my "hot pistol." I walked to his house, fully expecting another furring strip treatment such as he had given me in January for my exotic soup mixture. His wife opened the door and informed me that her husband was not home. With a sigh of relief, I turned the pistol over to her and, after an apology, I scrammed. The mere mentioning of the Gestapo made any German shiver. I was almost thirteen years old, and it would take a number of years for me to find out what they were capable of.

Any teenager growing up near a river was subject to its lure and danger. So, it came about that two of my classmates, both former KLV boys, and I decided to go for a swim at the river's edge. The day was hot and the old Rhine River flowed so peacefully, even with a war going on. We were swimming along the edge when we accepted a dare to swim across the river and back. We returned safe, tired and proud. The river was about eight hundred feet wide and boasted a strong current. When I told my mother what we had done that afternoon, she was shocked at first, but overcame her uneasiness with a joke.

There was little use in worrying too much over dangers because the air raids had increased to a 24-hour schedule. Power plants were high-priority targets. About sixty miles from us, the

Moehne power dam stood, providing electric energy for many defense plants. The British RAF attacked it several times. Since it was well defended and aircraft losses resulted the dam remained intact. Until - the one scary night when the dam was hit and a large area became flooded. It happened this way - the British concluded that conventional bombs were of little use. So they developed a torpedo bomb. A Halifax bomber (I've seen the aircraft in the London RAF Museum in later years, along with my British relatives) was converted to carry the "monster" in its belly. The torpedo bomb was released over the water and propelled itself many feet below water level toward the dam. The rest is history. The dam attack was part of a large-scale night attack on the Rhineland, so it was not apparent that the dam was the main target.

One of the participating bombers was badly hit over our home town. It proceeded to its death dive with all engines howling toward earth. I recall the terrified screams of all of us in the bombshelter who thought our end had come. Next morning we found the smoking remnants of a British bomber buried near the dam of the Rhine River. Three years later my father would have the job of erecting a gravemarker for the crew who had perished in the crash.

*Ludwig Wilhelm Knapp*

## Chapter 9

## Futile Hopes

In the second half of 1943 it became clear that the war would end in a German defeat - events on the Eastern Front and in North Africa made the finale quite clear. To lift our morale, our leadership talked about imminent "wonderweapons" that would turn the tide in our favor. Many young soldiers died believing and hoping that this promise was real.

The year 1944 was to be my last school year and also marked my induction into the Senior Hitler Youth (Hitler Jugend, HJ). We had a choice of the different branches. I chose the Naval Group. Our local group consisted of about twenty boys, fourteen to seventeen years old. We had regular weekly training meetings. At fourteen, I had a good knowledge of Morse code, semaphore with flags and the international sea flags alphabet. For training purposes, our group also utilized a large wooden boat manned by twelve oarsmen.

I remember one long trip, May 1944, for which our destination was the Drachenfels, the highest mountain in the Sieben Gebirge south of Bonn, on the Rhine River. It was sixty miles upriver; getting there was not a big problem. The Rhine is a major trade route, and at any one time you can spot a number of freight barges pulled by a tugboat upriver. The barges, connected in line to each other, are linked to the tugboat. Their load could be anything - at that time mostly coal. Since the clearance above the water line was about one foot, the barges could be boarded easily. One of our crew who boarded the barge tied its tow rope to the stern of the tugboat. Provided that we did not board the barge in order to cause mischief, we were received as welcome hitch-hikers. At night the tugboats dropped anchor and all traffic came to a halt. We slept at the river's edge under the stars. When our sleep was interrupted by the RAF, we had to find the nearest air raid shelter. The next day our upriver journey continued, and again we were tied to the freight barge.

I recall once when we had company: another HJ Naval group tied up with us. Since these fellows came from the City of Koeln

31

they probably decided to show us country hicks some tricks. They used a grating from the base of their boat as a water ski. The grating actually was made by nailing cross-wise a number of 1" x 4" by 2' x 3' boards. This base was tied to the stern of their boat, allowing for about a 10 foot slack. Another rope across the base provided a firm grip for the skier.

When the guy on the "ski's" began skillfully showing off his talents, Peter H. grew envious; he was manning our boat tiller at the time. It did not take him long to realize that the position of our tiller determined the balance of the skier. Ever so slowly Peter moved his tiller to the point where the skier lost his balance and found himself drifting down river. The hapless guy swam to shore and ran up river some distance ahead of us. He dove into the water and hoped to board our barge again. The swift river current, however, was too much for him and he missed our barge. He swam back to shore and then ran upriver again. At that point, using semaphore arm signals, he let his fellow crewmembers know that he was exhausted. Well now, the city boys had to untie their boat in order to rescue one of their own. And that is how some would-be water-skiers were sabotaged by a bunch of country hicks.

In the afternoon we reached our destination. We hiked to the top of the Drachenfels (Dragon's Rock) which provides a beautiful view of the Rhine and the nearby area.

On the return trip, the temperature rose and we found ourselves without sun lotion and drinking water. We applied a coat of margarine as substitute lotion on our bodies. It worked, but left a smell. After some hesitation, we scooped up river water to quench our thirst - somewhat risky but we survived.

One month after our river trip, our trusted boat, the "Herbert Norkus", named after a martyred Hitler youth, met a tragic end. During the summer months it was tied up at the river's edge; during the winter months, it was stored in the ferry owner's shed. Across the river from the tie-up spot was an oil refinery, needless to say, a military target.

It was on a bright summer Sunday, around noontime - I had just returned home from a HJ meeting. The sirens sounded and heavy bomb explosions followed immediately. Normally, after the siren's warning we would hurry at once to our air raid shelter.

However, on that Sunday our mother had prepared pork chops for dinner. She urged me to go to the shelter. My reply, "If I have to die today, it will be with the pork chop in my belly." After the all clear sound of the sirens, we learned about the raid's target, the refinery. A large "carpot" bombing attack had inflicted heavy damage on the plant. One of the stray bombs scored a direct hit on our boat, leaving us a mess of many wooden pieces strewn over a large area. Our Naval HJ felt bad about it, but soon afterward the events of the war would escalate to such a degree that we would no longer have had time for cool and leisurely river trips.

At this time I would like to tell you something about the Hitler Jugend. It was founded in 1933 immediately after Hitler became Chancellor of Germany. We were told to be proud, that we were the only organization to carry the Fuehrer's name. Yes, he had big plans for us. The program could be summarized as early military training. If this sounds strange, look at the history of the Boy Scouts. Their founder, British General Robert Baden-Powell, a Boer War hero, was convinced that his soldiers were individually inferior in ability to their enemies, the Boers. He concluded that early youth training would give the British soldiers a better chance for survival and victory.

Upon his return to England, Sir Baden-Powell started the Scout movement. Soon afterwards the program took roots in the USA. At the beginning of World War II, the U.S. Army needed officers in large numbers. Since the Army recognized the value of previous scout training, it offered all Eagle Scouts, the opportunity to attend Officer's School.

Adolf Hitler, ever-visualizing conquest, would add his own refinements to his Youth movement group. The unit was divided into the following branches: Air Force, Navy, Tanks, Signal Corps and Cavalry. Another group, added later, consisted of Firefighters. A need for them emerged when air raids raged over Germany, a phenomenon that our leaders had not foreseen at the beginning of the war.

During our junior years, at the ages of ten to fourteen, we received training in map and compass reading, as well as rifle training. Each senior group received specialized training. After a certain number of lessons, the student was required to pass a test in order to receive advanced training. Each member was administered group A, B, and C test, the latter being the most advanced.

Some of my older friends spent summer vacations in semi-military camps in order to receive extra training. Others spent time on board the Naval school ship, Horst Wessel, named after a martyred storm trooper. It is the same ship that was taken over by the U.S. Navy as a war prize. To this day it serves as the U.S. Coast Guard Training Ship, The Eagle. Some modernization features: air conditioning and female quarters. The "Horst Wessel's" future was certainly not envisioned by its planners.

Air Force training was conducted by the use of sail planes. If this sounds primitive, ask an older pilot about the value of flying sail planes and powered aircraft. The art of building small, hand-launched sailplane models was supported. Some of these models were propelled by rubber bands or mini-gas motors.

The group interested in the operation of tanks received training in diesel and gasoline engines. Signal Corps training provided phone and Morse code practice. The Cavalry group looked impressive, but their presence was soon neglected as training in more modern skills rose in popularity. All this training of Germany's ten-to eighteen-year-olds meant little or no juvenile delinquency or gang fights.

# Chapter 10

# What Indoctrination Accomplished

In 1946 my friend, Joseph Wierich, was interviewed by a friendly British Army Captain who happened to be the commander of the British Occupation Forces in my hometown. The Captain had gone to the Hitler Youth Home and looked at the archives. When one day he recognized Wierich as a "Junior Sailor" on a photograph, he asked Wierich to follow him, showing him the photo album and asking him about the group's activities. My friend did this and answered all his questions. The Captain remarked that British youth could have benefited from a similar program. He also expressed his amazement that neither fights nor gangs existed among the different groups. My friend replied, "We had an idol." When asked who that was, Josef said, "Adolf Hitler." End of chat.

I have another example of what indoctrination and early training can produce. During my hospital stay in 1946, I met Otto. He was in his early twenties but had a healthy crop of completely gray hair. He kept us entertained by telling us many jokes. When somebody asked him about his gray hair, he told us the following: Otto had attended Pre-NCO (Non-commissioned officers) School at sixteen years of age. After getting first class training and graduating from the school, was sent to the Russian Front.

The German Army used advanced foxholes in front of their main trench lines. They were used for listening posts at night or to destroy tanks. For these purposes, they had to be well-concealed. Otto found himself in one of these holes with a Russian tank bearing down on him. The enemy had spotted him and stopped his tank above the hole. The tank-driver usually would then go into the following maneuver: The tank would keep turning in complete circles, thereby neutralizing the enemy below him, either by sheer terror, paralyzing him into inaction, or grinding him into mincemeat. In this case, after a number of circles, the tank driver assumed that this enemy soldier was out of action and began proceeding toward the German lines - but not before Otto aimed a magnetic charge at the bottom of the tank! After this encounter, although Otto's hair turned color, he lived to tell about it, but not so the tank crew.

Otto finished the war on the operating table of an American Field Hospital. The surgeon, by removing many pieces of shrapnel, saved his leg. After closer examination, that surgeon discovered to his amazement that the projectile was a German mortar shell. How could he tell that? One piece of the removed shrapnel showed the German Eagle. When showing it to Otto and asking him what happened, the surgeon was informed by his grateful patient about the following: Otto's infantry squad was supported by a mortar unit. Unfortunately and mistakenly, this unit fired short and hit Otto's squad causing casualties. The bond between the members of Otto's squad was so strong however, that the survivors "took care" of the mortar crew.

In 1956 while attending the U.S. Army Engineering School at Fort Belvoir, VA. I met a fellow student, who was a Canadian Sergeant. When he learned of my background, he told me the following: As a young soldier in the Canadian Army, he had fought in Normandy. His outfit was opposed by units of the Panzer Division "Hitler Jugend." The division did not have any older soldiers in its ranks. Mysterious? Not really - for the following reason: It was felt that older soldiers would have had a negative effect on the fighting spirit of its younger soldiers. Those young Germans preferred to die before surrender, even in a hopeless position. This philosophy was no doubt the results of years of indoctrination.

One more example of youth indoctrination of a less serious nature - during my work with Habitat for Humanity in the USA: In the 90's, I met N.W. His mother had emigrated to the USA from Germany after World War 1.

In 1938 she decided to visit her home country. She took her son along - he was around 8 years old and an American citizen - to meet his cousins. N. noticed that his German cousins went to weekly meetings wearing funny brown uniforms and that they sang strange songs while they marched. When he expressed curiosity, they invited him to come and join the group. So it came to pass that Cousin N. from across the big water became an honorable member of the D.J. (Deutsches Jungvolk) the Junior organization of the Hitler Youth, and spent much time in front of a mirror practicing how to salute.

Shortly thereafter, when the clouds on the political horizon began to darken and war seemed imminent - his mother decided to return to the country of her choice, the USA.  It took much convincing on her part to impress on her son, N., to leave that "happy marching group" in the old country.  When N. related this to me - about his days in the 1930's - we both had a good laugh.

One of those leader-indoctrinators who began working in 1933 at the time of Adolf Hitler's take over was given the title of Reichs Youth Leader.  His name Baldur von Schirach.  Sounds like that of a real German with a title of nobility to prove it.  In fact, the name was bestowed upon him because his American born mother had been married to a German nobleman.  Baldur was educated at Harvard.  He had a knack for organization.  Besides his cool name he had poetic talent, and he certainly used it!  One of his poems went like this, in German:

Und wuerden wieder uns verbuenden
Sich Himmel Hoelle und die Welt
Wir wuerden aufrecht stehen und stuenden
Bis auch der letzte niederfaellt.

Translation:If heaven, hell and the world would unite against us, we will stand up and fight them until the last of us falls down.

My friend, the Canadian NCO, can certainly testify as to the effect of such poetry on the young minds who preferred to die rather than surrender.

In 1945 with the collapse of the Third Reich, the poet I have been describing, had a chance to practice what he preached to millions of German youth over the years.  Baldur von Schirach exempted himself from the "ordinary dying crowd" and chose to surrender quietly to the American Forces.  He was one of the war criminals seated in the 1946 Nueremberg docket.  The hangman was waiting for him.  But then a little surprise happened.  The American judge at the tribunal, Robert H. Jackson, was flooded with letters from the USA.  The letters were sent by the Daughters of the American Revolution.  They all pleaded that

Baldur von Schirach's life should be spared. Why? One of his ancestors was a signer of the Declaration of Independence. Anyway, the letter campaign worked; his life was spared and the newly galvanized German received a short jail sentence. The honor to die for the Fuehrer was left to the real Germans.

# Chapter 11

# In Depth Inquiry

For many years to come, people will ask, how could the German people have been deceived by Adolf Hitler and why did they follow him to the end? Due to worldwide depression, economic conditions in Germany were especially serious. Promises for change came from the extreme left, the KPD, the Communist Party of Germany and the extreme right, the NSDAP, the National socialistic German Workers Party, in short, the Nazis. Since reports about the "success" of the Communist Party in Russia did not favorably impress the German voting public, many Germans gave their votes to Adolf Hitler and the Nazis, but it was never a majority vote.

In 1933 Paul von Hindenburg was the Chancellor of Germany, a one-time World War 1 hero who at 85 years old was said to be going senile. He called Adolf Hitler and asked him to form a coalition government. The Nazis knew exactly what they wanted, and in their modesty, they asked only for the control of the interior department, for its police only. As a result, Adolf Hitler was named Fuehrer in January 1933.

In February 1933 the Reichstag Fire was set. The Reichstag is the equivalent of the Capitol Building in Washington, D.C. The alleged arsonist, a mentally disturbed communist, confessed. Hitler asked for and received emergency powers. Armed with legal far-ranging powers he arrested all those who opposed him and sent them to the first concentration camp, Dachau, near Munich in Germany. Here, the inmates were mostly Germans. Many rank-and-file opposition members were re-educated and then released. They would be told to change their old ways, to give the new party a chance and all would be forgiven. Most of the men had families to support so they promised loyalty in return for their release. As a result there was no further persecution against them by the Nazis.

Another group did not fare that well. The more determined ones received beatings by the "brown shirts" - some died and

39

others were kept prisoners for many years. Yes, our country had started on its way to "law and order," NSDAP style.

Among the unemployed was a large number of seventeen-twenty year-old men. They were soon put to work by the Reichs Arbeits Dienst, the new pick-and-shovel organization that would build the first sections of the autobahn. Since little mechanized equipment was used, this building project created work for many idle hands. The problem of funding all these projects was easily solved when the new government went off the gold standard and declared that the work output was their new standard. The ends will justify the means. Of course, nobody expected how it would end...

After two years in power, Adolf Hitler had not only impressed the majority of the German population, but had gained friends in France, England and the USA. In 1935 Winston Churchill stated that he envied Germany for having an Adolf Hitler. Two years later, Churchill recognized where all the new leadership led and stated "The German pig needs to be slaughtered." When, toward the end of World War II, the big three met at Yalta, Marshall Stalin discussed with President Roosevelt some of the details of the slaughter to take place. Winston Churchill listened aghast and stated to both of them: "Take me out and shoot me right now, I want no part of it." Then the two other leaders returned to their senses. Nobody in Germany knew that we had a "Godfather" in Winston Churchill.

One of my earliest memories goes back to 1935 at the home of my parents. The subject of a discussion was an election then taking place. The Saar area of Germany, among others, was impressed by Germany's recent progress. There was a growing trend to reunify with Germany. The area had been separated since World War 1. For this purpose the Saar area scheduled an election. It would be the only time that the common people would be asked for their opinion. The result was a participation of over 95% of the electorate and over 95% vote for reunification with Germany vote resulted. The reason: I heard my parents and their friends discuss what might happen if the people would not vote - or worse, a vote against the return. Obviously secrecy did not extend to how one voted.

By 1936 all private homes and businesses displayed the new German flag bearing the Swastika. If you valued your life, you would certainly display it on all required occasions. If you did not - you would be called in for questioning...The following was the official position: If you are not with us, you are against us. And anything could happen to you. The year 1936 witnessed anti-Semitic legislation in Germany. It left little doubt that any person of the Jewish faith would face a dark future in the country. The name of Hitler's party, the NSDAP, implies in its first word "national" a philosophy of hate against foreigners.

*Ludwig Wilhelm Knapp*

# Chapter 12

# The Scars of World War 1 and Its Aftermath

In many of Adolf Hitler's speeches to the people, he used the phrase: The November criminals. (By this he meant German people who pressed and negotiated for the end of World War 1, leading to the November 1918 Armistice.) Since some of those who favored peace were Jewish, he blamed the German defeat in World War 1 on the Jews. The fact that the German Navy had started to revolt in Kiel, a homeport, and that even the German general staff wanted to negotiate an end to the war, were hardly mentioned. The majority of the Jews saw themselves as Germans first and were loyal to the Kaiser.

Professor Albert Einstein was the highest paid scientist in Germany and could choose the subject he wanted to study. Many of the Kaiser's advisers were Jews. So were many of the leading industrialists and scientists whose contributions assisted the defense industry and who created valuable inventions. Jews also fought bravely in the ranks of the army in the fields.

When the USA in 1917 with its great manpower and unlimited resources entered the war, the Jews were among the first to realize that in the end, Germany would be defeated. By urging support for the Armistice, the Jews saved the nation from even greater casualties and from further destruction of the homeland.

These were the facts: By not speaking up for the Jews in the coming years, we would eventually have to pay a high price in blood and in the destruction of our country. By forcing the Jewish intellect to flee from Germany, Hitler unwisely supplied future enemies with a large number of valuable scientists, and thereby guaranteed Germany's defeat before the war started.

In November 1938 an unsuccessful bomb attempt on Hitler's life was made. At this time, he was making a speech to recall the beer hall putsch of 1923 in Munich. He was saved when he left before the bomb went off. Again, in 1944, when another bomb missed him, Dr. Josef Goebbels, our Propaganda Minister, stated: "On both occasions God's providence saved him to lead us."—it is ironic that God was pulled out of the closet every time it suited

Hitler's leaders, but certainly God did not have a place among our leaders at any other time. I'm quite certain that similar thoughts must have crossed the minds of many Germans in the fall of 1944 when the country entered the last and bloodiest year of the war.

# Chapter 13

# The Years 1944 - 54

<u>The Apprentice Work Shop</u>

It is said that a sailor always speaks well of his first job, so I must be somewhat of a sailor at heart. My hometown, Dormagen, was very fortunate that a Bayer plant took roots within its boundaries around 1916. The plant first produced war supplies. The plant was located within one mile of the Rhine River and the major highway that ran to Koeln and Duesseldorf. Its much larger sister plant, Bayer Leverkusen, was located about ten miles upstream and across the Rhine.

Over the years the plants provided the area and its people with a solid economic base. Their strategic locations meant easy transportation access to highway, rail and river links. The river could be used for processed water and waste disposal. The plant produced a variety of synthetic fibers and wool as well as sulfuric acid.

Since Bayer envisioned further expansion in the future, the firm decided to train its own craftsmen as well as laboratory technicians. The year was 1936 and for these purposes, a work or crafts shop and laboratory shop was built in Dormagen. The former was a solid brick and concrete building approximately 120' x 360'. The latter was a wooden structure, somewhat smaller than the workshop. It was unusual to see a laboratory built out of wood, probably a safety measure, if overzealous lab students caused an explosion. Every April, twenty-five new apprentices began their training at the site.

The basic education in the mid-1930's in Germany consisted of eight years of grammar school, followed by three years of vocational school, (one day a week) with a focus on the apprentice's choice of trade. Those who chose higher education left their grammar school at fourth grade for six more years of higher education, followed possibly by college training. At the age of thirteen, we had to choose what to do with our lives, not exactly an easy task at that "ripe old age."

45

Looking back at my life, at any decisive points, I was very lucky. This was from the start - My father happened to be on army leave from Russia. He suggested training in the construction trade, either as a plumber or electrician. After that, the choice was easy. Two of my close friends, Peter and Josef, already had begun their training at the Bayer Apprentice Shop. Peter started in 1943 as an electrician and Josef in 1942 as a repair mechanic. I felt I was in good company.

In April 1944, not yet fourteen years of age, I joined Bayer as an electrical apprentice. The distance of 1.2 miles to work was an easy walk. The craft shop had about seventy-five vises. They were solid and "custom fitted." To have the correct elevation, you stood on the side of your vise, put your chin into the base of your open hand, and at that point your elbow had to touch the top of the vise claws. Corrections for user height were made by the adding of wooden blocks between the bench top and the vise base; or if the apprentice was below normal height, he would stand on a grate to reach the proper height. When properly fitted, the height would allow the user to exert the optimum file pressure on the workpiece in the vise.

Yes, we spent a lot of time filing. In later years, one of my co-workers referred to a file as a German milling machine. We both had a good laugh. Besides the vise and an assortment of different files issued to each of us, we received calipers showing 1/10 of a millimeter or 0.004 of an inch, various squares, and other tools. All trades in the shop had to learn the basics in filing. Later we prepared for specialties: repair mechanic, lathe operator, tool and die maker, and electricians.

The shop was equipped with a welding shop, arc and gas, a blacksmith, lathes, planer and milling machine. Since there were six in our graduating class of 1944, who started with me, I was surrounded by familiar faces. The leadership in the work place consisted of three adults plus a third-year apprentice. He had to do the dirty work - more of that later.

Since most of my years of education took place in the Hitler era, all teachers, including the shop teachers, had to be Nazi party members - at least nominally. The headmaster, Herr Kraemer, was assisted by Herr Jungblut and Herr Schuetz. Each training day began with the customary loud "Heil Hitler," and then the filing proceeded.

Individual performance and progress was evaluated by one's performance curve. All work pieces that we produced were checked by the senior apprentice. Each piece was checked for measurements, tolerances, squareness and neatness. This was the practical part of the performance curve. The theoretical part consisted of a weekly report with a work piece sketch and hours spent on each work piece. All writing had to be printed, neatness counted high for the end score. Results were displayed on the curve every two weeks. By the way, none of the work pieces produced by us had any practical value to the Bayer plant. There was no other place in the area that took the training of apprentices as seriously as Bayer. To emphasize the point - consider the third year apprentice. He was at a location, an elevated podium, where he could observe all first-year apprentices. It was his job, besides checking our work pieces, to check on our dedication to our work. Our task was to work and not to talk. For those of us who found it hard to skip the talk, punishment would be generously dispensed. After all, there was a war going on. In the back of our shop, there was an air raid shelter under construction. For one hour after quitting time the offender would have to backfill the air raid shelter. Many of our group spent many hours at this type of recreation. I recall that our whole group had one evening backfill hour. That was enough for me! (No mechanical equipment - all back-filling work was done by shovel).

In case you wonder what kind of shelter we had, it consisted of oval concrete sections with a flat bottom about 8' and 4' wide. They were joined by tongue and groove joints and turned 90 degrees every 40 feet. It afforded a maximum of protection for a minimum of material and excavation. The shelter did have electric lights.

In July 1944, Herr Kraemer, our headmaster, left us to join the army. Since he was a Hitler Youth Leader, he was able to avoid the draft up to this late date in the war. He told us that after many pleas, his superior in the Hitler Jugend finally released him to join the army. Of course, that was the politically correct statement to make to us at that time. But the fortunes of

47

war had been turning against Germany since 1943, and we were doubtful about his statement. He left with his army unit for the Eastern Front, which was closing in on Germany's borders. He died in action.

Herr Jungblut became our new leader. He was older than Herr Kraemer. All of us took turns serving as his office help for a few days. One day when I was his helper for the day, he asked me to take a letter to another department. For this purpose I used the shop bike. After delivering the letter, I started to return to the shop. On my way, the air raid siren warned of approaching enemy aircraft. My inner voice told me to get into a shelter. Many of us were used to the daily raids, so we did not take the warning too seriously. This was summer 1944, and the Allied Forces prevailed over Germany. After the all-clear siren I proceeded back to the shop by bike. On the way I heard people say: "The Apprentice shop..." When approaching our shop, I saw the reason for all that talk. Our shop was hit by a bomb - the classroom which was located in the corner of the building had taken a bad hit. Needless to say, I considered myself lucky to have sought shelter rather than taking a chance. This could have been my last letter delivery. Well, only the good die young. The other apprentices were all in the "sweat equity air raid shelter," in the back of the shop and nobody got hurt.

During our first year, Bayer attempted to improve our communication skills. For that purpose they hired a learned professor from Koeln, Herr Prof. Hoch. For some time he gave weekly lectures and dictated notes to all the new apprentices, laboratory as well as crafts. On those occasions he used the classroom at the lab building. He presented a difficult program to us, which did not make him very popular with us. We all thought we were pretty good since we had finished school less than a year before. However, the weekly returned test papers showed poor results for most of us. So some guys thought of evening up the score. The professor himself provided that opportunity. (He might have tried to influence our political thinking by opposing our leadership, who knows.) To speak up against Adolf Hitler in 1944 in front of some 50 Hitler Youth members would be tantamount as treason, which is exactly what happened. One of the students relayed the professor's message to the authorities. Result: No more weekly lectures for us and a change of employment for Herr Hoch. He found himself in a group removing duds and live bombs, of which there were plenty, in the city of Koeln.

On the other hand, Herr Moews, our vocational school teacher, tried to give us a different message. It was July 1944, Germany was sending its rockets to London. (After the war, it became clear that the German intelligence system in England was pretty poor. As a result, speculation about the effect of our rockets were pretty rampant and wild.) So Herr Moews made the following statement that contradicted facts: "Even the building bricks are burning over there, so they will give up soon." He was well-remembered for his propaganda zeal, and nobody expected to see him as a teacher after the war...more of Herr Moew's later.

The Bayer Plant

The Bayer Plant at that time was part of I.G. Farben, not exactly a good name when records of war-time labor were made public in the years after the war. Like many plants, Bayer employed labor from the occupied eastern countries such as Poland, the Ukraine and Russia to fill the gaps left by the German Army draft. However, these people employed, both men and women, worked right alongside the German workers doing the same work unattended by military guards. Local farmers employed many of these workers as well, all without guards, and there was no problem except for one incident which left a painful memory.

There was a "No Smoking" rule in effect for the entire Bayer plant. It is no secret that many addicted smokers all over the world go to the restrooms to satisfy their craving. The Bayer plant was no exception at that time. What made the situation highly dangerous was the following: In order to save water, the toilets were of the dry type, all inter-connected, served by timed flushing. However, this hookup lent itself to the accumulation of sewer gas, which is explosive. So one day it happened, a cigarette butt or match caused an explosion that took the lives of eight workers. The tragedy left a painful memory. There was little doubt that in other areas of the German industry, eastern workers were mistreated. However, in my hometown there was fair treatment. As in all cases, again there were exceptions. I learned the following many years later. The local I.G. Farben Plant had many different production departments. The person in charge held a doctorate in chemistry and in most cases, the bosses were also members of the Nazi party.

Herr Dr. H. led one department that employed many foreign workers. It was 1943 and the fortunes of war were turning against Germany. Dr. H. developed a win-win policy of duplicity. He did the following: At the "visible level" of his production department he told his lower level managers to be rough and demanding toward the foreign workers in order to raise production. Even a kick in the behind was all right with him. Anything for the Endsieg (final victory.)

Then there was the other side of his thinking. In case Germany would wind up a loser, he did prepare for his future. He employed several foreign workers in his home as domestic help. He treated them well, and in return he asked them to verify in writing that he had treated them well.

Later in 1945, after the Allied victory he used those letters to prove that he was not a bad guy after all. However, his claim did not keep his name off the "community service" list; the person in charge saw right through him.

During my travels, in my later years in the USA, I met former eastern workers who had lived and worked in the Dormagen Bayer Plant. They had good memories of the place. They were especially grateful for the fact that being in Germany right after the war gave them a choice between returning to their former homeland or emigration to the USA. Needless to say, the ones who came to the USA made a choice for freedom and a better life.

In the summer of 1943 our local labor force was comprised of many men and women from the German occupied areas of East and Western Europe. They were soon to be reinforced by an unexpected group from the Southern part of Europe - Italian POW's. They came as a result of Italy's capitulation to the Allies and joining them. The former Axis partner was now a potential enemy. Italy was divided into the North Facist camp led by Mussolini, still an ally of Germany, in contrast to the southern part of Italy, led by Marshall Baddolio who was now an ally of the invading Western Forces. I recall the new workers at the local sugar factory wearing their Italian army uniforms. Yes, time was surely changing...

Meanwhile—back at the craft shop, the apprentices created their own excitement under somewhat more controlled conditions. All the students of the welding shop had their own practice table which was constructed of steel plates and pipes. We thought it rather funny to fill the pipes with welding gas then inserting a glowing welding rod into them. The result: a loud explosion that lifted the welding table in the air.

In the meantime, the "boys next door" in the blacksmith shop did not want to be outdone. They created little steam guns by plugging pipe fitted with elevated legs. After filling these pipes with water, the jokesters plugged them at the other end. When the window facing the road was opened, the guns with their lower-capped ends were placed into the smithy's fire and heated. As soon as the water turned to steam, the projectiles were on their way. With all the horsing around nobody got hurt - the Lord must have liked us after all.

*Ludwig Wilhelm Knapp*

# Chapter 14

# Life Changes as Germany Faces Defeat

After the June 1944 invasion of Normandy, life ran normal at the shop for a while. However, following the breakdown at Falaise in August 20, 1944, life was not the same any more. Germany's Western Front lines were disintegrating and very much in retreat toward the German borders. The Hitler Youth was called upon to shore up additional lines of defense for the army in addition to the west wall. Tank trenches, as well as infantry trenches had to be dug. Our shop life came to a sudden halt in face of this priority and we boarded a train to take us to the Netherlands, which was at the time occupied by Germany. We were quartered at Dutch farmhouses and slept in the barn on straw.

I had just turned fourteen years old in September 1944 and awarded of taking a more active part in the defense of the Reich. We participated in making a tank ditch near Venlo, a border town. I do not know whether this or any other tank ditch actually caused a serious delay to advancing tanks. Anyway, we felt useful for a while.

Then the government decided to concentrate on the defense lines of German territory so we "advanced to the rear" - the fancy term for a withdrawal. The army and HJ decided that the fourteen-year olds were a little too young after all. Both called instead for the formation of all the "young ones" as they asked for volunteers to stay on. However, to their surprise, all their prospects wanted to go home. So, we were accused of letting our soldiers down. Since almost everyone had a member of his family in the service, many of us changed our minds. We were individually questioned by an army officer who had lost one arm in combat asking whether we would like to stay. Since my father was serving on the western front, I did not like being told that I had let him down, and so when I was asked, I agreed to stay. The officer took a look at me and must have felt sorry for that "puny Hitler boy." He called the army truck driver, who drove the baggage truck, to take me along in his cab. Since all my friends had to take a lengthy march across the border, I felt their envious glances. Soon the truck was loaded and we left from the Netherlands for Kaldenkirchen, across the German border. Our destination was a large farm with a big storage barn. We arrived in the early afternoon. Later in the evening, the remaining marching columns joined us. Since it was air raid time, a complete black-out prevailed at their arrival. All of us sank dead-tired into the piles of barn straw.

We were in our country again, and it should have greeted us in a friendly way in contrast to how we were received by the Dutch farmers. However, our return did not turn out that way. During the black-out night, one fellow needed to relieve himself. He chose to do this in the hallway of the farm's living quarters. Needless to say the next morning the farmer's wife (her husband was probably serving in the German army) became quite upset. In her furor she said: "I'd rather have a hundred Russian soldiers here than ten Hitler youth." She was quoted to the chain of command. As a result, in the afternoon, a car pulled up. The farm lady was taken to Gestapo Headquarters. I can only hope that she survived the war.

It seemed that our operation leaders were not very decisive because the next day another offer to stay as volunteers was made to the fourteen-year old trenchers. This time there were no "stay appeals" made. So, among many others, I chose to go home. Since my friends, Peter and Josef and many others were fifteen years and older, they had to stay and remain active in the trenching.

After returning home, I continued work at the apprentice shop for some weeks. Since the older ones were away trenching, there were only the first-year apprentices left.

As the front lines retreated further, we received another call to man pick and shovels - this time closer to home. Our site was in the Kapellen area, about twenty-five miles from home (Dormagen). This time, everyone, young and old, was invited. We worked in teams of two. Our daily work was assigned us - a trench section of 11' x 3' x 5' deep. It was mostly flat farmland, so the work was not too difficult. Each crew had to finish its assignment, before we could return to our quarters, which happened to be a schoolhouse. (Based on our previous experience), somebody in charge was opposed to farmhouse quartering, maybe because the rest rooms were too remote. Our trenching work was supervised by Army construction engineers.

The American Air Force roamed freely over Germany's skies and any observed movement, day or night, was subject to attacks. I remember one night - when in the early morning hours the siren sounded its warning - we woke up, one guy sounded off ordering us to get into the shelter, another loud voice answered, "Oh, shut up!" Only moments later some bombs dropped nearby, and everybody dashed for the air raid shelter. The town Kapellen, in which we were stationed was under attack; some damage nearby did occur and even some roof tiles of our quarters went flying.

The attacks grew more intense during the day. At that time, we were out in the fields trenching. There was a railroad line nearby which connected to the front lines. The line was heavily used by ammunition trains. That morning, a moving ammo train was spotted by U.S. dive bombers and attacked. Some cars were hit and started burning - the flames caused rockets to ignite and they became airborne. As it happened, the rockets were of the "screaming mimi" type. Which meant, when ignited, they became airborne and on their way to the target, made a loud screaming noise. Those definitely ear-piercing vibrations were frightening.

That fine autumn morning we became the targets - when the rockets, out of control, happened to land a few hundred yards away from us. Fortunately our trenches were deep enough to give us shelter and we suffered no losses, but our ears rang for a long time afterwards. This was another close call - one of many.

We learned later about the fate of the ammunition train. While it was under attack, some cars started burning; however, the escort crew managed to disengage the burning cars and save Themselves and the train. Self-preservation makes heroes out of common men.

During the trenching activity, we had no toilet facilities. You had two choices: either time yourself to use the facilities in your quarters - or use the open field. One trencher, a little more modest than the rest of us, invented his own method of disposal. He went into the nearby completed trench section, squatted down and relieved himself. He was soon spotted and received a name change. His name, R.S., became S. the trench bomber. It stuck with him for the rest of his life.

The schoolhouse in which we were stationed had its classroom benches removed; the center section had two 4' x 4' wood beams on the floor and the area between beam and wall was filled with straw and covered with blankets for our nightly rest - when we were not disturbed by the British RAF. I cannot remember any fights between us trenchers. There were two possible reasons: One, we were too tired after hours of daily trenching to have any excess energy to use for fights among us; two, we were all from one section of Germany, the Rhineland; its natives have a reputation of being resilient and full of humor in contrast to some more "serious Germans."

There was no entertainment, hardly any radios, and the daily news reports about the war were getting grimmer from day to day.

I remember one fad of "entertainment". We were adequately fed to support our daily trenching powers. The food contained a lot of beans and sauerkraut, a mixture that produced gas. Somebody hit on the following idea: When we were in our quarters and felt that "gas flow" was eminent, we let it be known, lay down and stretched our pants bottom fabric. Somebody in the group then held a lit match to the bottom of the pants and, the body gas was converted into a cute little blue snake of combustion. We did not know that we were pioneers for the environment. At the time the clothing materials permitted such experiments. Today's fabrics may not be so tolerant and could cause personal injury to the jokesters.

We all had some personal belongings with us. There was no privacy and everybody knew what you had. Theft among us was very rare. However, as in any situation there are exceptions. At the early stages of trenching in Holland, our friend named C.B. saw his opportunity, or so he thought. He accumulated a horde of things from the belongings of his friends. They soon became suspicious and observant. As a result, C.B.'s crime was discovered - he was caught with the goods and identified as the thief; then chased and severely beaten. I did not see this finale but I was told by the eyewitnesses that the pursuers drove him into the upper beams of the high storage barns. After, they shaved his hair off, he was a marked man for some time. This was the only case of theft during our trenching months, from September 1944 to

January 1945. By the way, C.B. did not return to the apprentice shop but chose to continue his work at a local shop. The barn episode may have had something to do with that.

*Ludwig Wilhelm Knapp*

## Chapter 15

## Search for Replacements

As the war continued and German army losses mounted, the leadership had to become more creative to attract replacements. One method of doing this was turning to the Hitler Youth. There were millions of fourteen-sixteen-year-olds available who could be used by the army in non-combat jobs to free army personnel for front line duties. I experienced the following: In December 1944 I had a chance to enroll in Army Signal Corps School located in Solingen. I accepted, since I hoped for some electrical training because my goal was to become an electrician. So, after Christmas of 1944, some of my friends from my hometown and myself, reported for one month's training. Solingen was located about twenty miles from Dormagen (but across the Rhine River; this town is known all over the world for the high quality of its steel products).

Under Army signal corp's teachers, forty of us were to become skilled as both radio Morse code and field phone operators. At least that was the plan, but there was a little change along the way. A few days into our training we were told the following: We are going to have an officer from the Signal Corps of the Army visiting us tomorrow. He will tell you that you can serve as a volunteer helper by moving signal equipment by truck to the front lines. You will be asked the following "Do you want to become soldiers?" And you will answer, loud and clear - "Yes, we want to become soldiers."

Again, since I was only fourteen years old, I was not asked, but my hometown friends left and went on to become junior soldiers. One of the two, F.S., was the son of a local hero. His father had gone to school with my mother. In his mid-twenties, that was around 1932, he became a member of the local S.S. unit.

In the thirties, there were over thirty different political parties in Germany fighting over the leadership. The dominant ones, the Nazi and Communist party, fought bloody and often deadly battles. In one of these incidents F.S. died. After Hitler's takeover in 1933, a monument in F.S.'s honor was erected. At the anniversary of his death, yearly ceremonies took place. Now his

59

son was asked to put his life on the line. Luckily, he survived the war in good health. This was not the case of many other "Junior Soldiers."

The following incident from World War II was revealed by an American news reporter following President Reagan's placing of a wreath at Bittburg, a German military cemetery in 1985. Our President Reagan wanted to place missiles on German soil to counteract the placement of Russian missiles. For this purpose he wanted the good will of German Chancellor Kohl. He got what he wanted from the Germans, but a lot of negative reaction arose in the American press, since the cemetery contained many SS graves. The reporter traveled the cemetery area. He needed lodging and food, so he frequented a local inn. During his meal, he talked to the innkeeper who told him about his own wartime experiences. He was fifteen years old at the time and a member of a trenchers group numbering 150. They were individually approached by SS officers. A friend of his told the officer that he wanted to join a certain Army Regiment since several generations of his family had served in it. The innkeeper told the SS officer: I already volunteered for submarine service. Both replies were accepted. The rest of the trenchers group, 148 in all, were turned into junior SS men. After the war the innkeeper tried to find some of them. He had no luck. It is anybody's guess as to what happened to them. War is cruel.

Another case of "recruiting" hit closer to home. My cousin Franz Josef Gesell was sixteen years old at the time he received an order to appear in front of his local draft board. His hometown was Neuss, about ten miles north of my hometown. At the end of his physical examination, he found himself summoned to a doctor sitting at a table. The doctor had a folded paper and asked him to sign it. Franz Josef was young and trusted authority. After signing it the doctor unfolded the papers, showed it to him and shook his hand: "Congratulations, you have just volunteered for the Waffen SS." When he got home and revealed his experience with the draft board, his father was quite furious and called him Himmler. In case you do not recognize the name, Himmler was Heinrich Himmler, the notorious commander of the Waffen SS. I'm sure you will find more of him in any history book of World War II. Of course, the name-calling was only done within the family. After all, you wanted to live and see the end of the war. There was a shortage of soldiers, but never a lack of police.

Luckily my cousin survived the war in good health, even to play the role of the goalkeeper in his local soccer club; he married and had a family. After years of work he decided to take a trip to Russia. He did not like the border-crossing inspections. On his return to West Germany he told friends and relatives about Russia. Soon they called him "the Red." When he decided to return for a second trip to the USSR, he decided to do something about the unpleasant searches by the Russian border guards. He contacted the closest Russian Consulate and requested a monthly propaganda magazine which he promptly received (There was little demand for it). After packing for his return trip he placed the magazine atop his suitcase contents. When he arrived at the Russian border, the guard spotted and grabbed the magazine, did not give it a second look, and went straight to his superior, who glanced at the cover, recognized it and chewed out the guard for giving a good Communist trouble and ordered him to let the traveler pass without any further search. I guess it is safe to say that my cousin had learned a thing or two since his appearance in front of his draft board at the age of sixteen.

Meanwhile, back to January 1945 at the radio school. The army instructors were trying their best to turn us into Morse Code geniuses. At the end of the month we were able to send and receive thirty letters a minute. After completion of this course, I returned to my hometown. At that time, I did not dream that my knowledge of Morse Code acquired at the German Radio School would someday be used to train boy scouts, including my son, in my after-the-war life, in the USA.

By February 1945 I found myself back at work at the Bayer apprentice shop. With American troops working their way towards the Rhine River, daily air raids increasing after a failed last offensive at the Battle of the Bulge, most of us realized that the war that Germany had started would soon end in defeat.

At the beginning of March 1945, the plant shut down and our home area became a combat zone. The local militia or Volksturm was called and armed. It consisted of very young sixteen-year-old boys to sixty-five-year-old men. This group would retreat across the Rhine River to Duesseldorf in order to reinforce regular army units to make one last stand. Sounds like General Custer - German style.

At this point my close friend, J.W. had received his draft notice with several other friends in the fall of 1944. They were told to report for the Arbeitsdients (work service) in March 1945 but, due to the military situation, their orders were changed to: Become members of the Volksturm (militia).

They had received a minimum of military training for what they had to face in the coming weeks—if you needed a definition of the words, "cannon fodder"—this was it.

My friend, Peter and I, paid a visit to an army weapons trailer after dark and stole a lueger pistol to give our departing friend, J.W. Our friend, J.W. left with his unit for Duesseldorf and to our surprise - he was back at his home two days later. Nobody asked questions. Many years later, our friend filled me in about his missing days. He told me the following: After arrival in Duesseldorf there was much confusion and he realized that he was unwilling to become just another casualty to prolong a lost war. He convinced several hometown friends to join him. The risk was great since it was difficult to get away. They chose to walk along the right side of the Rhine River (the German side), upstream toward Dormagen. They succeeded to get to the Dormagen-Monheim Ferry.

The ferry captain, the Piwipper, as he was called by the locals, recognized the hometown boys and gladly ferried them back out of harms way. They all made it safely home. Many years later, J.W.'s friends thanked him many times for inviting them to go with him for the stroll along the river in those critical days in March of 1945.

When some of the diehard Nazis from their unit found they were missing, they swore they would hang them upon their victorious return to our hometown. However, at this time my friend had the last laugh - he is still very much alive at the age of 74 with many bumps along the way.

# Chapter 16

# The Last Days of War

When the sound of artillery fire came closer with the approaching front lines in 1945, we all moved into our air raid shelters. Most homes had sturdy shelters with thick concrete walls, as well as steel beams and five-inch concrete ceilings, which gave good protection unless they were targeted as direct hits.

In the morning hours of March 5, 1945, American Infantry units, after short fire fights, occupied Dormagen. All homes displayed white flags, in the form of bed sheets. Most all of the former Swastika flags were later turned into kitchen aprons, the red base was very suitable for it.

Right from the first day of occupation, the American town commander turned my parents' home into his headquarters; it fit the following requirements: It was located at the main road Koeln-Duesseldorf, large and new (seven years old) and you could see the dam of the Rhine River. My family was asked to stay in the basement. Having your home loaded with G.I.'s brought advantages, but also disadvantages. The Ami's, (short for Americans) as we called the G.I.'s gave us food. And we were the first to be able to go through the trash pile which provided us with many "treasures." More of that later.

Occasionally, German Artillery fired a round into our town from across the river with minimal effect. Every home preserved food for the winter months. For this reason, one could find shelves filled with empty or filled mason jars, and ours was no exception. We were somewhat shocked when we learned that some of the G.I.'s had used these jars to relieve themselves during the night. Years later I realized they were unwilling to take unnecessary chances. They had come a long way from Normandy to the Rhine.

During the war all food supplies were rationed. Nobody went hungry. Obesity was an unknown word. Our leadership kept us lean and mean. The Allied Air Forces dropped copies of food ration stamps over Germany hoping to raise havoc with the food distribution. However, the copies were of poor quality, and anybody attempting to use them was promptly executed.

During my daily scrounging through garbage piles, put out by the G.I.'s, I looked for food, cigarette butts, and anything else that could be eaten, traded or used. One item that I treasured was a pair of combat boots which were a little big on me, so I grew into them. They provided me with decent footwear for many years. At that time, my fellow Germans invented another type of footwear, later known as the Ho Chi Min sandals, made from worn out truck and auto tires, flat rubber and straps. Those provided sturdy, well-vented footwear during the summer months.

Trash piles and the areas around my home were "blessed" with cigarette butts. After the butts were stripped of paper and the burned section removed, the clean tobacco was collected, weighed and repacked. It was a desired item for trade for some years. Five ounces of tobacco fetched six eggs or some bacon.

Before Easter 1945, I found a can that was slightly dented, but it showed a picture of plums. My mother was happy for the find, and she served it with our Easter pudding. When we tasted the pudding we discovered the "plums" were actually olives. Since we could not read the English label, our minds played this trick on us.

One day I found some Napalm-type hand grenades in the trash. Being young and unafraid, I went to the G.I.'s and turned the live grenades over to them. The G.I.'s seemed surprised and happy about the find.

After two weeks of occupation by our new "landlord," we were asked to move into another vacant apartment down the street. There was no shortage of living space in our town since many people had fled with the German Army. It was up to each individual to decide whether to stay in his or her home or apartment or flee and take a chance with the retreating army.

The U.S. Army had a non-fraternization rule with Germans in effect, but that was mostly ignored. Some of my friends, who had learned English in middle school, were eager to try it out, and many Ami's gave them a chance.

A number of vehicles left by the Germans were usually missing key parts like batteries, etc. The G.I.'s loved the challenge of getting the vehicles to move again for their own amusement. There was this half track in good condition, but its batteries were missing. Quite a challenge. One of my older friends who spoke English was having a conversation with a soldier who asked him for help. The soldier needed two large batteries. Guenther knew just the place for batteries. A little dangerous—but available. At the same time, an abandoned German tank was sitting at the edge of town somewhat elevated and clearly visible from the German side of the Rhine. The soldier asked us to go on a "mission" with him, and since we were young and dumb, we were the right helpers. Three of us followed him as he drove his own army vehicle, a truck. Guenther directed him toward the tank, just down the road a bit, but not too close to invite German artillery rounds. We carefully approached the tank, removed the batteries and returned to the truck. Everything went smoothly. The batteries were quite heavy. The soldier and I carried one, and my friends carried the other. Halfway back to the truck, the G.I. noticed that the battery was very heavy for his young helper, so he turned to me and asked: "Sommer es mol nieder setze?" The question was in my father's hometown German dialect and meant: "Should we take a break?" Hearing these words spoken by a G.I. in the same German dialect as was spoken in my father's home area, the Pfalz, had a profound emotional effect on me at this time. The soldier must have been from the Pennsylvania Dutch area. Hearing him made me wonder if my father was still alive and if he was wondering about how we were doing. The experience left me stunned.

Another dead vehicle incident, however, had a severe impact on my family. Before the war, my father had been self-employed as a stone mason. To get to the job site and move supplies and finished products, he used a motorcycle and a trailer. The motorcycle was sitting in his workshop - a G.I. spotted it and tried to use it. No luck, but he was not to be discouraged. After he spotted a nearby automotive repair shop, ₁ he pushed the motorcycle to the shop and asked the owner to fix it in exchange for cigarettes. The shop owner knew the motorcycle and its point of origin. However, the lure of American cigarettes overcame any reluctance he might have had. The motorcycle "disappeared" and as a result my father found it difficult to conduct his trade when he returned after the war in June 1945. Needless to say, my father was angry at Herr H. for fixing the motorcycle.

After living two weeks in the neighborhood apartment, we were told to move again. The house which contained our apartment was also needed by the U.S. Army. I believe we were the only family in town that the Army asked to vacate twice. Since it only required a minimum of things to take along, moving had little negative impact on my family.

The second apartment, which used to belong to the former local Chief of Police, was still well within walking distance of our home. Both apartments were equipped with all necessities because the previous occupants had left everything behind. The thought that the war would soon be over and life would improve made such disruptions more bearable.

The first few months of occupation saw food shortages, due to supply and transport breakdown. The most desirable jobs were to be found at our local farms because the farmer provided food at their table in exchange for your labor. Luckily we had a friendly farm lady, Frau M. living across the street who could use some help. After a few weeks of local farm work, Frau M. recommended me as a helper to her parents who ran a small farm in Anstel, about eight miles from my home. I returned home on weekends only. The friendly farmer always sent some food for my mother and sister.

During those weeks of farm work, I saw the daily air fleets of U.S. bombers bringing the war to an end.

# Chapter 17

# At the End of the War

The war's end was somewhat accelerated by an unexpected speedy crossing of the Remagen-Rhine River Bridge. In later years I learned that the first U.S. Infantry group to cross that bridge was led by a German-American sergeant who was born not too far from that bridge. Truth is stranger than fiction.

The war ended May 9, 1945. The mail had been interrupted for four months since January, nobody in town knew anything about the fate of family members who had served in the German Forces.

In June 1945, still at work as a farmhand, I received word that my father had returned - hard to believe, but to our joy, it was true. He had been called with the first draftees in August 1939, and now he returned as one of the first, in June 1945. Slowly life went back to normal, but we were off to a bumpy start.

There was plenty of reconstruction work waiting, but the needed building materials were hard to get. I had hoped to work with my father in his construction business - but after giving that some thought, his advice was "Finish your electrical apprenticeship at Bayer because there is little cement and other material available, I will have a tough time myself."

I followed his advice.

During the war years the plant and our town had received only minor bombing damage. There was much speculation about why the plant and town were spared. I do not wish to elaborate on speculations since my writing only reflects on the facts as I remember them.

Our first job at Bayer was to rebuild the bombed classroom. Two plant masons were assigned to lay the bricks, and we served as their helpers. At first, the helpers consisted of a first and a second year apprentice because the third and fourth year apprentices had been drafted during the last few months of the war. It took longer for these young men to return (by that time the classroom was finished), and some did not return since they had died in action.

I am still amazed at the zest with which we rebuilt the classroom. We made the work into a contest, to see who could carry the most bricks on the shoulder board, and who could carry the most up a ladder. It was easy to exceed our own weight, since the war years had strengthened our "physical frames and weight."

Since most large cities suffered heavy damage, principally caused by bombing raids during 1941 through 1945, the rubble heaps were extensive. The workload seemed insurmountable. Help came from an unexpected source. Just as the USA had Rosie the Riveter to contribute to final victory, the West Germans had the Truemmer Frauen (rubble woman). Thousands of women contributed greatly to the fast clean-up of the rubble heaps in the cities. Bricks were cleaned of their old mortar, and neatly stacked for recycling.

Food and fuel rationing continued, but the allocations were less than during the war years. May 1945 to May 1948 were the most demanding years with little food available; we also endured rationed electricity, sickness due to food shortages, and a rampant black market.

Thanks to American leaders such as President Truman and General Marshall, the U.S. by deciding not to play into Stalin's hand, saved Europe.

The USA initiated the Marshall Plan to the tune of sixteen billion dollars - it started the major funding for reconstruction of Western Europe, including West Germany. Since the dollars allotted to West Germany were jointly administered by the U.S. Army and the Germans, no money was wasted or lost. The results were better than in other countries.

When the first shipments of American corn flour arrived, this product was something completely new to us. Being unfamiliar with it and not knowing anything about its nourishment value, someone concluded the Ami's wanted to turn us into canary birds. We joked about it, but the corn flour was eaten gratefully.

When we returned to resume work at our shop, we had a complete set of new leaders. Herr Voigt was our new headmaster, supported by Herr Novak and Herr Kazmarek, all very capable people without a Nazi party past.

The schools in town underwent a "management change," and many teachers lost their jobs since their past was tainted by their membership in the Nazi party.

We were expecting similar changes at the vocational school level, but due to the shortage of qualified teachers, there were exceptions. One such exception was our first year teacher, Herr Moews. Every one of our faces showed surprise when he showed up and continued to teach. After all, we all remembered him as an outspoken party member. For an explanation, he tried to sell us the following line: "My promotion was blocked and I was one step away from being sent to a concentration camp." None of us were ready to buy his story. So my friend, J.W. stood up and said: "Come on, Herr Moews, we all know your past." Herr Moews had the gall to go to Herr Voigt, the headmaster, and complain about my friend's remark. When, later on, Herr Voigt assigned the shop graduates to different departments, my friend J and some of his friends found themselves sent to the powerhouse, a physically demanding job. This puzzled me, but even many years later, my friend insisted that it was a result of J.W.'s making that remark to the Vocational School teacher, Herr Moews. Be that as it may - J.W. ended his career at Bayer as a group leader of twenty Greek pipe fitters of whom he spoke highly, praising them for being hard workers.

*Ludwig Wilhelm Knapp*

## Chapter 18

## Return to Routine and New Signs of Industrial Growth

When mechanical work at the shop resumed, the routine changed due to the needs of the plant. There were a large number of rail freight cars sitting idle for sometime, requiring maintenance before they could again be rolling stock. We were assigned to get them ready. There was also a need for locks and bolts. Due to shortages of all kinds, replacements had a way of "wandering out of the plant." A joke circulated about the "wandering out" items. It went like this: There was this large industrial plant, where shortly after the war one fellow found an anvil, which was just what he needed at home. He brazenly put the heavy anvil on his shoulders and walked through the plant gate. A watchman stopped him to ask him what he was doing with the anvil. The fellow looked straight at the watchman and replied "Oh, I wonder who put that there?"

Many workers got to work by the use of a bicycle. However, tires and inner tubes were also in short supply and impossible to find. Some boy thought of a substitute - heavy ¾" or 1" I.D. waterhose; the hose was joined to a piece of cable and mounted on the rim at the valve hole by using a ¼ inch bolt. This innovation afforded an unusual ride, but there is an old German saying: "A bad ride is better than a good walk."

When winter came, there was an immense shortage of coal for heating homes. The townspeople soon found a kind of remedy. Daily coal supply trains shunted to the local industry usually in the evening hours. When the trains slowed down to a crawl, they were boarded by many brave souls who lightened the load by throwing coal or briquettes overboard, which were rapidly retrieved.

In comparison to other towns, Dormagen was better off since besides the Bayer Plant, we had a brewery since 1895 and a sugar plant built in 1864. Needless to say, the landscape in our country was generously "sprinkled" with a number of breweries. Ours

71

supplied the Koeln area with its products.  At the time, the quality of the beer left a lot to be desired, but today it enjoys an excellent reputation.  As part of the brewing process, some waste in the form of mash remains.  The local farmers can feed this to their cattle herds.  During one of my return visits to my hometown from the U.S., we had the chance to observe one of those herds.  My wife remarked that she had never seen such a relaxed and happy herd of cattle.

The history of sugar production goes back to the time of Napoleon.  The British Navy, during the war with Bonaparte, had successfully sealed off France and the rest of Europe by means of a blockade and thereby prevented the import of any supplies of cane sugar from the Americas.  The search for a substitute led in the utilization of beets as a sugar source  Beets had been used as a winterfeed for cattle.  The fertile soil in our area produced a good crop of sugar beets year after year.  When the sugar was extracted for human consumption, the process first recovered no more than 5% of the raw beet.  Over the years that figure rose to near 20%.

Another byproduct targeted for human consumption was the sweet syrup extracted from beets.  During both world wars, this syrup was an important food source.  The beets could - and were widely used - as a source of alcohol.  Much of that alcohol found its way to the black market.

Industrial plants at the time used hard coal exclusively. Residences were heated by coal, coke and briquettes, a soft-type coal.  Following the first years after the war, selling coal was the country's only way to obtain any hard currency.  So it sent its "black gold" from the Ruhr area to other European countries.  The coalmines played an important part in Germany's recovery.  This was largely possible by ignoring the orders that Hitler in April 1945 gave to Albert Speer, the famous architect, and to his army generals to destroy the coalmines.  Hitler wanted to deny any life continuance for the German people after their defeat.  There, orders that took priority caused shortages for the common people, which forced them to rely on "self help".  Needless to say, since coalmines ranked as top priority for manpower, sometimes unwilling men were turned into coal miners.  There was a miner's draft board dispensing regular physical exams comparable to the

way that the army draft board of the past operated. Many
unwilling candidates ingested "funny substances" to affect their
heartbeat or blood pressure so that they would be declared unfit
for mining.

*Ludwig Wilhelm Knapp*

# Chapter 19

# Surviving in the Midst of Shortages

At our plant we had a lunchroom where a thin soup or "something else" was ladled out in exchange for ration stamps. We all sat on wooden benches to which a table was attached. There was just enough room to seat three workers side by side. One busy day a fourth person asked those already seated if there was any room for him. Some kind soul answered, "Oh, sure we will make room for you, and in a few more months five of us will fit on this bench."

By this time everyone in Germany knew what a food calorie was - 1 gram of sugar equaled 4 calories and 1 gram of fat equaled 8 calories and everyone was hard pressed to get additional calories above the 1500 calories allowed per day. This was due to shortages and black market.

The Western European calorie allotment was one-third higher than that of West Germany.

No matter the black humor, ingenuity, substitutions, etc., the shortages took their toll. An increasing number of people became sick, since our bodies had little resistance. Pretty soon poor nutrition affected me personally. Illness started with nightly sweats, and I was diagnosed with tuberculosis of the lung in the beginning stage.

Over the last two years, I had a good friend Peter E., with whom I had spent many hours playing, even sleeping next to him during our trenching time for the army. Unknown to me at the time, his father and two sisters had their lives cut short by TB. Peter must have been a carrier but did not show it. Anyway, our plant doctor ordered me to rest for a few weeks, and then I returned to work.

Shortly afterward, I came down with appendicitis, and so my appendix was promptly removed by our local surgeon, Dr. Gilliam. I did not know it at the time, but this turned out to be a lucky incident. Before releasing me for work, he examined me, found me unfit, and sent me to a specialist in the City of Neuss, who verified that my TB required treatment. There was little hope for speedy recoveries at the time, but again a lucky chain of events took place in the fact that Dr. Gilliam, the surgeon, had consulted with the plant doctor, Herr Schmidt, at the Bayer Plant.

Today, in retrospect, I firmly believe that the Bayer plant, with its deep social concern for its workers, saved my life. The time was late 1946 and some of the plant workers were returning from Russia's POW camps. Their physical condition, after years of war and captivity, left a lot to be desired. The plant management would not accept them in their weakened state. Here was their course of action - Bayer owned its own hospital in Gross Ledern, a scenic, wooded and hilly area twenty-five miles north of Koeln. It was run and staffed by Bayer medical personnel. I was the youngest patient (sixteen). The former POW's now back in Germany had a large variety of ailments. Bayer fed them with food that was much better than the rationed food available to my parents. At first, there was no effective medicine; however, at the end of my three months' stay, the first medication developed in the USA for my illness was dispensed to me. Bayer must have acquired it through its worldwide connections. Up to that point, the only antidote was the "lying down care": Get plenty of fresh air and rest and eat good food.

I recall one of the many friendly nurses who had been with the German army in Russia. She now had a permanent reminder of that time: signs of frostbite on her nose. Bed space in the hospital was much in demand and so there was a shortage of it. A female M.D. was in charge. She determined when someone was ready to be discharged, depending on his medical status - and one other factor. How much did the patient participate in the healing process? I took every opportunity to get as much fresh air as possible, even when the weather turned cold. This fact was observed by our attending nurses and proudly reported to the female physician. She must have liked what she heard, because one day she hugged me and called me "an old fresh air fighter." She kept me at the hospital as long as she could. So as a result of three months' home rest and three months' Bayer Hospital stay, I felt I had a new lease on life and after some weeks, returned to the apprentice shop.

I had in those previous months gained some thirty-three pounds and grown a few inches as well. Some of the people at the plant hardly recognized me. I now continued my training at the electrical department of the plant, repairing appliances and overhauling motors. This was done under the watchful eyes of Herr Meister Victor Herter. He also gave the apprentices weekly lessons in electrical theory to reinforce our vocational school knowledge. We were all grateful for his interest in us. Soon we joined the journeymen electricians to serve as their helpers and acquire installation experience.

I was around seventeen years old. The food shortages persisted while the black market flourished. Frequently my father worked as a stone mason for farmers. That should have given us some extra food, had their promises to pay been kept. The reality was far different. I recall one evening at suppertime when my father had been given a can of sausage meat by a farmer customer. The top of the can showed a bulge, a sure telltale sign of its spoiled contents. On closer inspection my stepmother decided that it did not seem that "bad yet". Consequently she served it. My sister, about fourteen years old at the time, was hungry or brazen enough to ask for a second helping - remarking "If I do get sick, I want to go fast." My stepmother's judgment was correct - it was not our last meal.

Another day, the word on the street reported good fishing at a certain spot at the edge of the Rhine River. In those days, environmental rules were nonexistent, and the Bayer plant discharged its waste into the river via a concrete channel of about one-mile length. There were days when the waste contents were more toxic than usual, and as a result fishing near the discharge was affected. The dead fish floated in circles in this area. After a crowd of people gathered, equipped with long netted poles, caught the floating fish, they investigated them. The gills were squeezed open; a reddish gill meant the fish was fit for the human food cook pot; a white gill was designated for the chicken-food cook pot. Thus, there was nothing wasted. The reader might shake his or her head at this recklessness, but there was no case, to my knowledge, of a man or chicken becoming sick as a result of eating the questionable catch. Hunger will drive one to take risks.

Today, strict rules are in effect and obeyed. There is a tank filled with live fish in the Bayer plant's main office building. Through it passes the plant's daily river discharge. If any fish go belly up, the discharge is corrected. Better a few dead fish than a dead river.

At times during my walks through the woods, I was lucky enough to find dead rabbits caught in sling traps. They also became welcome additions to the daily meals.

After the resumption of mail service between the U.S. and West Germany, many families in Germany received care packages. These packages contained a wide variety of foods, clothing and usable items not available to the German population from 1945 to 1948. If your family could not use a gift from abroad, you could easily trade it for something you needed. We were fortunate enough to have two of my father's brothers living in the USA. We were the recipients of many such packages which helped tremendously. I recall one time we received something looking like chocolate. A little taste convinced us otherwise, because it turned out to be chewing tobacco. I knew a man who chewed tobacco, who ran a store with electrical supplies. A deal was struck and we were able to get a replacement for a broken appliance plug.

Our neighbor, the family of W.E. received regular care packages from Belgium. The source: During the war years, Herr E. had a coworker at Bayer from Belgium. Herr E. made it a habit to bring a sandwich in for him and hide it every day at a predetermined place because this practice was against German rules. The grateful recipient remembered Herr E. after the war when their fortunes were reversed and Herr E. and his family could use some help.

Another source of care packages was France. Herr E. had fought in the German Army in World War 1 and during the course of the war, he became a POW. As prisoner, he learned some French.

In 1940 some French prisoners worked in Dormagen and Herr E. befriended one of them and helped him in many ways. The former French soldier, Louis, did not forget that. When Louis returned to his country after the war, he mailed packages to Herr E. and the families kept in touch for many years.

Needless to say, pretty soon a number of stories circulated pertaining to care packages and their contents. Black humor, envy or other reasons must have prompted the tales. Here is one

I remember. There was this lucky family who received a steady stream of care packages from the other side of the pond. Each item had been carefully labeled as to contents and necessary instructions by the American side of the family. So, all went well and the recipients were very grateful. Then came the day when a package arrived containing a mysterious unlabeled can. The family put their heads together and decided it must contain food seasoning. So it was used in the preparation of their daily food - used for potatoes, vegetable gravy and meats. It was soon consumed.

Shortly after that point, the family received another package with a letter. The writer stated: "By the way, the last package contained Aunt Mary's ashes, she passed away recently and she wanted her ashes to be buried in the old country. We hope you can do that - sorry, but we did not label the can"—Truth or fiction, you be the judge. If you ask me, there is a saying, "Truth is stranger than fiction."

Here is another story for your perusal. There was this little town somewhere in Germany and the year was 1946, one of the hardest after-war years. The town baker was doing his best to provide the townspeople with bread. But try as he might, there were days when he had not enough flour to make the required amount of loaves for his customers. He knew of a "flourstretcher" that had been used in many countries when times were difficult. He decided to use sawdust to obtain the needed bread. Nobody noticed his "new ingredient" until the day when a baby was born with a wooden leg. If you have a problem deciding whether this story comes under truth or fiction, I suggest you take Biology 101.

As the food shortages continued, they took their toll. This was especially true for young people. We had a total of four cases of lung TB in our apprentice shop. One of the victims was my friend, Peter E. whose entire family, except his mother, had died (from the same illness.) Peter was about eighteen years old when he died. His mother died of grief caused by the early demise of her husband and all her children.

Peter R. had returned from the army after some time in a French POW camp. After he was diagnosed to have TB, Bayer sent him to its hospital in Gross Ledern. Besides him, there was another apprentice infected by this dreaded disease. It seemed that if you inherited a predisposition for TB from your parents, your chances of survival were few. Since I was not genetically "cursed," I was the sole survivor of the four in our shop—or does the saying "only the good die young" apply in my case?

The black market dictated our everyday life. Hourly wages were low and had no relationship to the prevailing black market prices. The money printed under Hitler was still in circulation and considered useless. The average hourly wage in 1947 was RM 3.00. The black market asked RM 21 for an egg and RM 60 for a pound of sugar. In order to survive people resorted to both legal and illegal activities. As a result the police had their hands full, but lacked heart to pursue every infraction.

I can relay a personal experience. After my TB hospitalization discharge, my parents sent me to my grandmother for another few weeks of rest. My suitcase contained a few pounds of sugar and a pair of attractive shoes (U.S.) to give to a lady who would help toward my support. Her town was located in the French occupation zone whereas I came from the British zone. Legally, such travel required a special permit, but it was seldom enforced.

After some hours of travel on dark tracks and trains, I realized that I had missed my transfer point. The trains stopped for the night at that time. We passengers left to spend the night in a waiting room. After a few minutes in the room, I noticed the doors blocked by plainclothes police searching for black marketers. When trying to leave the room, I attracted their attention. One of the plainclothes men asked me over and started to question me. Apparently he must have liked what he heard - after looking him straight in the eyes and telling him the full truth, I gained a friend who advised me how to get to my grandmother's home the next day.

Among all the holidays in Germany, there is one that is celebrated like no other in my home area of the Rhineland. That holiday is Fastnacht, also known as Mardi Gras or Carnival. It has greater meaning in predominantly Catholic areas around the world: Rio de Janeiro, New Orleans, Muenchen and Koeln.

Since Koeln is my home area, let me describe the steps of the celebration. It starts annually on November 11. The number 11 stands for something crazy. At its climax, the holiday is celebrated with great zeal for three days previous to Ash

Wednesday. Beginning in November, the days are marked by a heavy schedule of masquerade parties, discussions of the previous year's events, silly speeches, dancing, drinking and parades with floats. The celebration leaves an unforgettable memory. To preserve the memory, each year brings forth a new harvest of carnival songs. Some of these tunes fade away fast, but others become hits and endure. One of the lasting songs dealt with the subject of the Hitler-time government. The moral of the song: "We are going to be very reluctant to follow any government without many questions. It does not matter what our future leaders look like, whether they sport a mustache or beard, eyeglasses or bald pate (in reference to Hitler and three other Reich leaders), You made monkeys out of us for too long, and that is not going to happen again." This song surely made a lasting impression on all of us.

Another hit song referred to the illegal activities, mostly committed in the name of daily survival. In it the words stated: "In two years we will be all equal because every one of us will have a police record."

Many of the daily offenses involved the production and distribution of Schnapps (whiskey). Since my home area could boast many farms growing sugar beets, it was also the site of many moonshine stills that produced a popular and easily traded item for the black market.

*Ludwig Wilhelm Knapp*

# Chapter 20

# Turning Point

Finally the year 1948 rang in. We did not know it, but it was the turning point. The same year brought several positive events. The most far-reaching was the Berlin blockade by the Russians. It was countered by the Allied Airlift, that, at great expense to the Allied in money and life (some 77 lives of transport crew) about two million people were supplied with fuel and food. This action profoundly changed the attitude of the German population toward the Allies. Former enemies had turned into friends upon whom you could count. I'm sure it brought into memory the promises made by the German Air Force Commander Goering to supply German Army troops stationed around Stalingrad in 1942. Those attempts failed, and the course of war on the Eastern Front was reversed. In contrast, this Allied airlift grew in numbers and efficiency to a degree that the Berliners lacked for nothing. As a result, Stalin called the blockade off.

During the last few months of that blockade, West Germany was allowed for the first time to elect its own post-war government. It was led by Chancellor Konrad Adenauer. He was up in years, but also very capable. He had been Mayor of Koeln until he was removed by Hitler in the 1930's. Suspected of involvement in the assassination attempt on Hitler's life in 1944, he was arrested and placed into a concentration camp. Only a man of destiny could have survived. Reinstated as Koeln's Mayor by the British occupation forces, he lost his office again when he incurred the anger of the British. Next he became the national leader of the CDU Party, the "Republican Party" of West Germany. He ran for office at the first election and was elected Chancellor in 1948. Needless to say, a great task faced him, but the "old timer" met the challenge. Beloved by the Germans and highly respected abroad, he became one of the country's best leaders in a time of great challenges. One of the first steps enacted in his term of office was the creation of a postal stamp called "Emergency Contribution Berlin." It helped to defray the cost of the Airlift that had been mostly underwritten by the Allies.

In May 1948 the newly elected German government enacted currency reform. Every person in West Germany received DM 40 from the government. The Hitler currency, the RM, was all declared null and void. The reader might question how could that change ever work, but work it did. The German situation was unique and required deft decisions.

The Minister of Economics, as the office was called, was filled by Herr Ludwig Erhard, a heavy cigar-smoking jovial Bavarian. He was up to the challenge. The story goes that he was met in his office on the historical day by General Lucius D. Clay, who was at the time the U.S. High Commissioner over West Germany. Expressing his concern over the change to Herr Erhard, Clay said, "My experts tell me the currency reform is not going to work." Herr Erhard looked at the high commissioner and said: "Do not worry," flicking his ashes off his cigar, "My experts tell me the same thing." The new currency looked like a relative of the U.S. dollar and indeed it was. The new government, when first contemplating the changes, was very concerned about the danger of counterfeiters if the plates to print the new money were produced in West Germany. It asked for American help and received it. Result: The new DM was printed in Washington, D.C. at the U.S. Mint. That was the reason for the similarity between the U.S. dollar and the newly issued currency bills.

In April of 1948, I suffered from a bad cold which possibly could cause a TB relapse. The good plant doctor, Herr Schmidt, sent me to Muenster Eifel, another Bayer resort, for three weeks. He did not like to see any reverses in one's health, and the danger of a relapse was eliminated.

The money reform had an immediate and great positive effect. The black market disappeared almost overnight. Food rationing ceased. All types of food and goods began to appear and were for sale. Since there was only a limited amount of money in the hands of the people, hoarding did not become a problem.

The Bayer Company took bicycle orders from its employees; a manufacturer was contacted and a discount deal was made. Soon everyone was riding a new bike to work, the purchase price being deducted through payroll deductions. The disappearance of plant water hoses stopped. The need for "ersatz" bike tires ceased to exist.

Of course, the best part of the reform was the new availability of all kinds of nourishing food which brought about a healthier, disease-free population.

After three years of poor living conditions, we witnessed what seemed like questionable reform producing improvement that exceeded our highest expectations.

*Ludwig Wilhelm Knapp*

# Chapter 21

# Progress of my Career as Electrician

Due to my days' off for illness, it was to be expected that the completion of my apprenticeship would be delayed. However, in the fall of 1948, I was fit and was permitted to take my electrician's test. After passing the test, I joined the electrical crew in Workshop E. The E stands for electrical as you might surmise. The total work crew consisted of forty electricians, four apprentices, three Meisters, two Time calculators plus tool storeroom attendants and office clerks.

It was our job to maintain and install new electrical equipment at the plant. At the time three to four thousand people worked in many departments, some at round-the-clock shifts. In the shop a friendly atmosphere prevailed among workers and management. Our starting wage was around DM 1.25 per hour which was not very much. However, by working accord (see below), we could add another 33%.

Wages at the Bayer Plant were higher than what other local industries or contractors paid their people. Bayer was a desirable place to work.

Herr Lagenbucher, who was one of the leading engineers and the plant CEO, had spent time and studied in the USA before the war. He took the accord system from the USA. It was the art of pre-calculating industrial mechanical work. The theory involved estimating the amount of time needed to complete a job. For instance, if a certain job took 100 minutes, we must aim to complete it in 82 minutes. That amounted to 18% savings; to that sum was added the prospect of earning another 15% if you worked under the accord condition. The result in efficiency added up to 33% which translated to an addition in your base wage. The outcome: a busy efficient workforce rewarded by good pay.

In my later years, working as an electrician in the USA in the early 1960's, I did not find the accord system applied. However, times changed in the mid 1980's when the US industry embraced an economizing trend. Then my German accord training came in very handy and assured me job security.

I continued my work at Bayer until the summer of 1953 when my Uncle Ludwig from the USA visited us. He was my father's brother who had emigrated to America in 1928. After describing life and work in the USA, he offered to sponsor me should I decide to emigrate there. His words awoke a wanderlust in me, and I decided to leave.

I had several advantages over my two uncles when they left Germany decades before, having a good trade and some knowledge of English. Also there was no economic depression in America as there had been in the 1920's. Besides, I could live in my Uncle Ludwig's home.

After his visit I mailed my application for emigration to the U.S. Consulate in Frankfurt, West Germany. While waiting for a response from the U.S., I continued work at the electrical shop.

In May 1954, I took a test to enter our plant Fire Department since I did not know whether or not I would receive a visa. Acceptance into the fire department was followed by six weeks of intensive training at the Bayer Plant in Leverkusen. Four of us commuted daily by bus. We had to rotate jobs to know each other's job. Besides daily lectures, training films played a part in our education. Some of the films had been made during the Third Reich. Since training had not changed in regards to fire fighting techniques, the films were still in use. They all had one thing in common: since they were made in Hitler's time, the exercises ended with the Heil salute that prevailed at the time of filming. When we saw the salute the first time at the end of the film, we laughed out loud. The West German youth of the 50's did not exactly identify with the cannon fodder of the 1940's.

Our trainers were experienced fire captains who had served our plant during the war years. One particular captain told us that the sprawling plant, hundreds of buildings, were not bombed during the almost six years of war. Why: I leave that to your speculation. There was a glaring exception - the structure that produced rocket fuel, and I offer my theory. After Germany's daily rocket firings at England, German launching sites and fuel launching sites and fuel itself became prime targets of the Allied Air Forces and, as it happened, only the Bayer Plant structure producing rocket fuel was promptly bombed and destroyed. The German captain I refer to had actually witnessed its bombing by the U.S. Air Force in 1944. We will get to the opposite of the scale later in the book. (See Dresden air raid in Part Two.)

Soon we became more and more proficient in our daily fire-fighting exercises. At the end of each exercise, the troop leader was required to account for all men and equipment requisitioned and report the number to the captain. Our bosses liked our progress, but there was one thing lacking. Our clicking of our heels and our military salute were too sloppily performed, and we were told that much. So I decided to satisfy the troop leader once and for all. I alerted my fellow trainees about my plan to assume the role of troop leader.

All went well to the end of the exercise when it came time for my report. But first, I faced the captain, clicked my boot heels and raised my right arm to the vaunted Hitler salute. He became quite p...off and proceeded to chew me out. I received prompt and unexpected help from one of my Dormagen friends who remarked: "But that is exactly what you showed us in the training films." Our troop-leader promptly stopped dressing me down; our sloppy nonmilitary reports became acceptable from that day on. The source of my unexpected help came from my friend, Olaf N., a native of Berlin, whose inhabitants are known for their humor and quick wit.

One phase of the training for the fire-fighting duties consisted of exercises in a tear gas-filled room while wearing an air-back-pack. If the buzzer on a personal pack indicated a near-empty tank of oxygen, its wearer was disqualified. The consumption of too much air implied that the trainee was physically weak, and therefore he would be rejected.

After the completion of our training, we joined the Bayer Plant Fire Department in Dormagen. Our job hours were 7:30 AM until 7:30 AM. The time was divided into eight hours work in one's respective trade, plus 2 hours of night watch. We were assigned a certain watch route, using a bicycle to reach all the checkpoints of the large plant. The remaining hours were for free time and sleeping. Of course, that could be interrupted by a plant fire alarm, in which case we would go into action. In contrast to our sister plant, Leverkusen, which responded to an alarm almost daily, owing to its huge size, our plant in the early 1950's might have had only five fires a year. As a result of that, we left the plant at 7:30 AM, well rested with twenty-four hours' free time. I used this time to work in my electrical trade on my own or to work in my father's busy concrete shop.

# Chapter 22

# Invitation from Abroad

In September 1954, just when my routine was established, I received a letter from the American Consulate in Frankfurt, inviting me to appear for a physical examination. In earlier years this was done when one arrived at Ellis Island, N.Y. Now it was conducted in the resident country of the visa applicant. As a result, no more tears were to be shed at Ellis Island - in my humble opinion, a change for the better.

All applicants had to fill out extensive questionnaires to reveal the facts of their life in regards to school, training, political past and medical history. In my case, I was checked very thoroughly because of my earlier bouts with lung TB. To my relief, I was declared healthy and received the much hoped-for visa to the USA.

Shortly after this I gave notice at Bayer and informed them of my intention to emigrate. On receiving my news, some of my former bosses were not too happy, since they liked to retain their skilled people, but I was told: "If you do not like it there, come back to us."

After my father took me to see my grandmother to say goodbye, I took leave from my family for an uncertain future across the big water. The means of transport in the 1950's was mostly by steamer before the idea of air travel gained rapidly. I left from Rotterdam, Holland in October 1954 destined for New York, USA, traveling on a former troopship, now owned by the Holland American Line. The steamer ticket cost was around DM 700 or 3 month's pay. The good ship was the "Groote Bear" of approximately 10,000 tons. It carried beside myself a small number of other German immigrants bound for America after a smooth journey of ten days.

*Ludwig Wilhelm Knapp*

# Appendix

My Fathers's Home Area

Baumholder → US-German US ARMY Trg Area

Ottenbach → Fathers Birth Place

Etzweiler Vacations

Large US Air Base

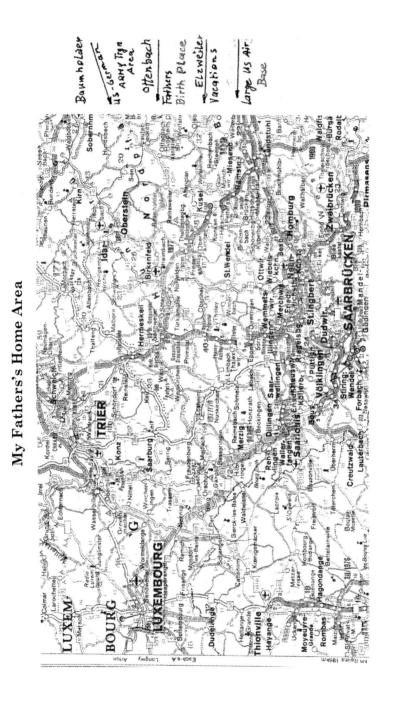

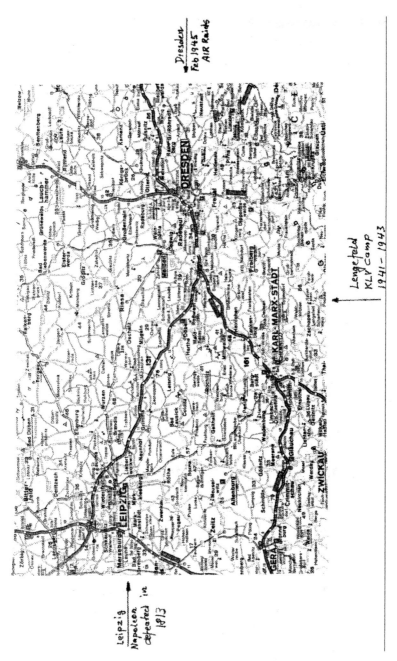

**Figure 1East Germany**

Arnhem Sept 1944
One Bridge too Far
101ST Airborne

My home area.

Wesel - Matd 45
Last Airborne
Drop in WW II

Venlo Sep 44
Trenching

Kaldenkirche

Trenching
Sept 44

Duesseldorf

Neuss

Dormagen
Iome Town.

Leverkusen

Koeln

Aachen
Nov 44
1ST German City
to be occupied.

Kapellen Nov 44
Trenching

Field Trip

**1942 Yearly sport contest winners.**

**Day Room**

**Camp Leader**

**I and my babysitter, Wolf - 1931**

**My Stepmother, Me, Sister, Father - 1943**

**KLV Camp Gym**

**KLV Camp, Main Entrance**

**Winter 1941 -42**

**Summer 1942 - No excess weight**

**In Summer Uniform 1942**

**In Hitler Youth Uniform - 1944**

**Our Home at 153 Koelner Strasse**

**KLV Camp 1941**

**My Mother and Me - 1934**

**My Father - 1940**

*Ludwig Wilhelm Knapp*

WESTERN CAMPAIGN SONG

Kamerad wir marschieren im Westen mit den Bomben
Geschwadern vereint. Und fallen auch viele der
Besten, wir schlagen zum Boden den Feind.
Vorwaerds, voran. voran ueber die Maas ueber
Schelde under Rhein marchieren wir siegreich
nach Frankreich hinein.

meaning --    Comrade, we march westward, united with the
              bombing squadrons. And even if we loose
              some of our best, we will beat our enemy to
              the ground.
              Forward, forward, let us go across the rivers
              Maas, across the Schelde and Rhine, we march
              victorious into France.

U-BOOTE    (Submariners song)

Heute wollen wir ein Liedlein singen, trinken wollen
wir den Kuehlen Wein, und die Glaser sollen dazu Klingen
denn es muss geschieden sein. Gib mir deine hand, deine
weisse hand, leb wohl mein Schatz, lebe wohl den wir
fahren gegen Engeland.

meaning -- Today we will sing a song and have a glass of
           cool wine, as the wineglasses clink together
           we have to part. Give me your hand, your white hand.
           Farewell, my dear, farewell. Now we will part
           on a voyage against England.

EASTERN CAMPAIGN SONG

Von Finland bis zum Schwarzen Meer vorwarts nach
Osten du  stuermend Heer, Freiheit das Ziel
Sieg has Panier, Fuehrer befiehl wir folgen dir.

meaning --   From Finland to the Black Sea forward to the East
             you attacking Army - freedom the aim, victory to
             the flag, leader give orders, we follow you.

106

FALLSCHIRMJAEGER LIED    (Paratroopers Song)

Rot scheint die Sonne, fertig gemacht
Wer weiss ob sie morgen fuer uns auch noch lacht
Schieb an die machinen geb vollgas hinein
Startet los flieged an heute geht es zum Feind
In die machinen, in die machinen Kamerad da gibt es
Kein zurueck, Fern im Westen stehen dunkle Wolken
Komm mit under zagenicht komm mit.

meaning --   The sun shines red, get ready
             Who knows whether the sun shines for us yet by tomorrow
             Get the transport planes ready, give full throttle
             Start up today we will meet the enemy.
             Into the planes, into the planes, comrade there
             is no going back.
             For in the West there are dark clouds.
             Come along, come and do not hesitate.

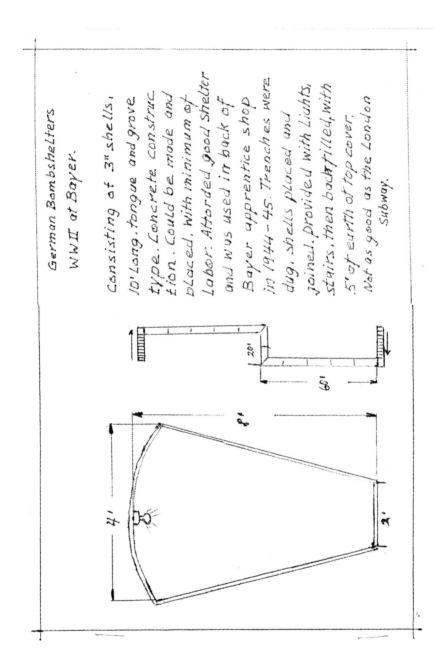

German Bombshelters
WWII at Bayer.

Consisting of 3" shells,
10' Long. tongue and grove
type. Concrete construc-
tion. Could be made and
placed, with minimum of
Labor. Afforded good shelter
and was used in back of
Bayer apprentice shop
in 1944-45. Trenches were
dug. shells placed and
joined. provided with Lights,
stairs, then backfilled, with
5' of earth of top cover.
Not as good as the London
Subway.

*Postwar official weekly Food rations - Adult* (handwritten)

# Die Lebensmittel-Zuteilung

Für die 1. Woche der 79. Zuteilungsperiode (20. 8. — 26. 8. 45) wird folgendes aufgerufen:

| Ware | Verbrauchergruppe | | | Je Abschnitt g | Auf die Abschnitte |
|------|------|------|------|------|------|
| Brot | Normalverbr., Teilselbstvers. Butter, Teilselbstversorger Fleisch/Fetten | E | Roggenbrot Weizenbrot | 500 500 | 42 41, 43, 44 u. 20 Kleinabschnitte *Bread* |
| | Vollselbstversorger | E | Roggenbrot Weizenbrot | 500 500 | 42, 43 41, 44, 45 u. 20 Kleinabschnitte |
| | Normalverbr., Teilselbstvers. Butter, Teilselbstversorger Fleisch/Fetten Vollselbstversorger | Jgd | Roggenbrot Weizenbrot | 500 500 | 42, 43 41, 44, 45 u. 20 Kleinabschnitte |
| | Normalverbr., Teilselbstvers. Butter, Teilselbstvers. Fleisch/Fetten | K | Roggenbrot Weizenbrot | 500 500 | 42 40, 41 u. 20 Kleinabschnitte |
| | Vollselbstversorger | K | Roggenbrot Weizenbrot | 500 500 | 42, 43 41, 44, 45 u. 20 Kleinabschnitte |
| Butter | Normalverbraucher | E Jgd K | Butter | 82,5 | 73 u. 16 Kleinabschnitte *Butter* |
| | Teilselbstversorger Fleisch/Fetten | E Jgd K | Butter | 5 Kleinabschnitte a 5 g | |
| Nährmittel | Normalverbr., Teilselbstvers. Butter, Teilselbstvers. Fleisch/Fetten, Vollselbstvers. | E Jgd | Nährmittel | 100 | 16, 17, 18 |
| | Normalverbr., Teilselbstvers. Butter, Teilselbstvers. Fleisch/Fetten, Vollselbstvers. | K | Nährmittel | 100 | 16 |
| Käse | Normalverbr., Teilselbstvers. Butter, Teilselbstvers. Fleisch/Fetten, Vollselbstvers. | Jgd K | Käse | 62,5 | 81 *Cheese* |
| Kaffee-Ersatz | Normalverbr., Teilselbstvers. Butter, Teilselbstvers. Fleisch/Fetten, Vollselbstvers. | E, Jgd, K | Kaffee-Ersatz | 100 | 79 |
| Speisekartoffel | Normalverbr., Teilselbstvers. Butter, Teilselbstvers. Fleisch/Fetten | E, Jgd, K | Speisekartoffel | 1000 | 61, 62 *Potatoes* |
| **Für die ganze Zuteilungsperiode (20. 8. — 16. 9. 45):** | | | | | |
| Zucker | Normalverbr., Teilselbstvers. Butter, Teilselbstvers. Fleisch/Fetten Vollselbstvers. | E | Zucker | 250 | 26, 27 *Sugar* |
| | Normalverbr., Teilselbstvers. Butter, Teilselbstvers. Fleisch/Fetten, Vollselbstvers. | Jgd K | Zucker | 250 | 26, 27, 28 |
| Marmelade oder Zucker | Normalverbr., Teilselbstvers. Butter, Teilselbstvers. Fleisch/Fetten, Vollselbstvers. | E | Marmelade oder ½ Zucker | 500 250 | 28 *marmelade* |
| | Normalverbr., Teilselbstvers. Butter, Teilselbstvers. Fleisch/Fetten, Vollselbstvers. | Jgd K | Marmelade oder ½ Zucker | 500 250 | 29, 30 |
| Puddingpulver | Normalverbr., Teilselbstvers. Butter, Teilselbstvers. Fleisch/Fetten, Vollselbstvers. | K | Puddingpulver | 2 Pck. a 50 g | 21, 22, 23 *pudding* |
| Vollmilch | Normalverbr., Teilselbstvers. Fleisch/Fetten | K | Vollmilch | ½ Ltr. tägl. | M.-Bestellschein |
| Entrahmte Frischmilch | Normalverbr., Teilselbstvers. Fleisch/Fetten | E | Entr. Frischm. | ¼ Ltr. tägl. | E.M. Bestellschein *Milk* |
| Entrahmte Frischmilch | Normalverbr., Teilselbstvers. Fleisch/Fetten | Jgd | Entr. Frischm. | ¼ Ltr. tägl. | E.M Bestellschein |
| **Für die 1. Woche (20. 8.—26. 8. 45):** | | | | | |
| Fleisch | Schwer- und Schwerstarbeiter | | Fleisch | 50 g | S/Bst 113 und 114 *Meat* |

Schwer- und Schwerstarbeiter erhalten weitere Zulagen für die 1. Woche der 79. Zuteilungsperiode über die Zusatz-Ergänzungskarte 79/1, deren Abschnitte mit festem Mengenangaben versehen sind, gegebenenfalls zum Teil durch die Betriebsküche.

**Anmerkungen:**

1. Auf den Abschnitten 41 der E-, Jgd- und K-Karten sowie auf alle Abschnitte der SV-, SV-Jgd und SV-K-Karten kann an Stelle von 500 g Weizenbrot = 375 g Weizenmehl abgegeben werden.

2. Auf den Abschnitt K 42 und SV-K 42 können für die Kinder bis zu 1½ Jahren (bei Altersnachweis durch Geburtsschein oder Familienstammbuch) an Stelle von 500 g Brot = 375 g Kinder-Getreide oder Kinder-Reis-Nährmittel abgegeben werden.

3. Für Kinder bis zu 1½ Jahren kann unter Verzicht von 1500 g Brot die Milchration um täglich ¼ Liter erhöht werden. Die K-Karte (Normalverbraucher und Teilselbstversorger in Fleisch und Schlachtfetten) muß in diesem Falle der Kartenstelle zur Entwertung der entsprechenden Brotabschnitte und Ausgabe eines Milchbestellscheines vorgelegt werden.

4. Betr. Lebensmittelkleinhändler:

Etwa vorhandene Restbestände an verderblichen Waren, wie Butter, Margarine und Käse sind dem Ernährungsamt sofort mitzuteilen.

5. Bezugsschein-Ausgabe an die Lebensmittelkleinhändler Dienstag, den 21. August 1945 beim Ernährungsamt, Kanalstraße 14.

Neuß, 17. August 1945.

*250 g = 10 oz* (handwritten)

Der Oberbürgermeister
gez.: Dr. Nagel.

| Hl. Dreikönige | St. Konrad |

*Ludwig Wilhelm Knapp*

# Part Two

# The Rest of the Story

What Happened to My Town, My Friends and My Family on
Return from War and their Tales of Survival.

*Ludwig Wilhelm Knapp*

# Chapter 1

# History of my Hometown in Germany

Dornumagus was the Latin name for firewood. When you look at a map of today's Germany, you find it located between the cities of Koeln and Neuss next to the Rhine River. Its modern name is Dormagen, a city of approximately sixty thousand inhabitants.

Today its two major industries are its Bayer plant and EC, a crude oil refining plant that produces gasoline and chemicals.

There are many traces of human inhabitation during the Stone Age found within its borders. However, actual development started in the first century A.D. when Roman wagon trains travelling between the early towns of Colonia and Novesia used Dornumagus as a stopover, mainly because it provided an abundance of dry wood for campfires. At that time, Roman legions had occupied a large part of the area that is now called Germany.

It is a fact that the PAX ROMA (Roman Peace Treaty) was a fact of history because the inhabitants of the territories it affected benefited greatly from the Roman presence. Water, roads and provisions protection were some of the major improvements introduced by the Romans. It is also true that an outstanding citizen of the conquered region could rise to the position of a Roman CAESAR. Let the best man rule Rome was a theory that was taken seriously. There was no prejudice practiced. To prove it, note that the Roman senate elected Septimius Severius, a North African, to be one of its Caesars. This black leader served from 193-211 A.D. However, not everyone agreed with the Romans. The notable exemptions were the Scots and the North Germans. Hadrian solved the Scotch problem by constructing a wall across the width of England, over ninety miles in length. The project was a success - it made it possible for the Roman legions to succeed in defending the largest part of England against the north invaders, "the pigs," as the Scots were called at the time. A grateful Rome elected Hadrian, the wall builder, to be its Caesar. He ruled from 117-138 A.D.

As in England, the population held different opinions about the Romans; the German tribes felt likewise. Among the tribe leaders of the northern part of Germany was Armin the Cherusker. He was able to unite its northern tribes to fight Rome. He chose the time and place of battle - the rainy season and densely wooded areas, which are today's Teutoburger Woods. When a large armored Roman force marched through the muddy forest roads, the ambushers were ready for them. The attackers had mostly hidden in trees, and they rained arrows down on the surprised Roman legions, destroying them completely. When the bad news reached Rome, CAESAR Augustus (9 AD) moaned, "Varus, Varus, give me my legions back," to no avail, for Varus, the Roman legions commander, had committed suicide by his own sword after his army was defeated.

In the 19th century the Germans built a monument in Westphalia in honor of Armin, the leader of the battle in the Teutoburger Forest.

Before they began work on the Statue of Liberty, their American project, the French designers visited the German monument in order to study its form and its method of erection. American GI's after World War II held the Westphalian monument in low esteem. Apparently they did not like the image of an oversized German lifting his sword high into the air, so they used the statue for target practice. Since only small arms were used, the statue could later be restored.

After the heavy losses in Germany, Rome reconsidered its strategy against the northern area. It recognized the two largest rivers, the Rhine and the Danube, as its borders. Since these two rivers were large obstacles, they could be easily defended at that time. Another aspect of the new Roman defense strategy resulted in the formation of the German Legion, or as the Romans called it, Legion Germanicus. This Legion consisted of German mercenaries who were paid by Rome. Even then "Fight fire with fire" was a desirable guideline. And where was that Legion stationed? It can be said with certainty that it was at Dormagen, based on the many artifacts that were found when excavations for new construction took place in my hometown, both in the past and present. There are historical experts today who will tell you that

if England would have used the Roman system in its battles with
its American colony, the U.S. would still be British today.

My town was occupied by the French under Napoleon who had
declared "You do not have to pay taxes to the church anymore; you
now pay them to us." He not only raised taxes but also took
German draftees for his Grand Army. Soon he started his eastern
adventure - he marched toward Moscow, only to be driven back by
the Russians. Soon they were joined by the Prussians and other
nations who put an end to Napolean's designs at the Battle of
Leipzig in Saxony. Cossack units drove the French from
Dormagen in 1814. The next foreigners to occupy Dormagen were
the British troops both after World War 1 and after World War II.
In my early childhood my mother told me about the good
relationship my hometown inhabitants had with the Tommies, as
the British soldiers were called.

After World War 1 ended, millions of German soldiers
returned from the front to a defeated homeland. Since the Kaiser
had fled to Holland, monarchy rule ended. In its place, many
factions tried to convince the people of Germany that their ideas
were the best. The 1920's brought a turbulent time to Germany -
unemployment and inflation as well as the 1923 attempt by Adolf
Hitler to take over the government in Munich, Bavaria. The loyal
state police of Bavaria did not tolerate the early marchers of the
NSDAP (The Nazi Party), as it was called. Sixteen members of
that group lost their lives, and many others were wounded. Ten
years later the sixteen dead were declared martyrs of the Third
Reich and honored by a national holiday on November 9. One of
the earliest propaganda songs was dedicated to them. Among the
wounded was Hermann Goering, the same man who later became
Reichsmarshall and Commander of the German Air Force, the
Luftwaffe. His wounds were severe and he would have bled to
death had he not been saved by two sisters who dragged him off
the street and nursed him back to health. Some thirteen years
later when the anti-Semitic laws were enacted in Germany,
Goering remembered his rescuers and acted accordingly. He
helped them leave the country. Yes, the two ladies were Jewish;
so there was even some good in Hermann Goering.

At that time, in 1923, Adolf Hitler was arrested and sentenced
to three years in jail at Landsberg. One of his fellow inmates was

115

Rudolf Hess, who later became his deputy or vice chancellor. While incarcerated, Adolf Hitler dictated his book "Mein Kampf" to Hess. In it he outlined his plans for the future which should have been a warning for things to come, but foreign leaders and the German people did not take him seriously. They based their beliefs on his earlier years, viewing him as a drifter, soldier and now as just another radical party member.

After Hitler's rise to power in 1933, the book was given to every German couple after their marriage.

# Chapter 2

# My father, Karl Knapp

In the fall of 1943, somewhere in the center section of the Eastern Front, my father's unit came under attack by Russian planes. While he was undercover, his leg was struck by a heavy timber section, requiring hospitalization. He did not know it then, but it was one of the luckiest days in his army life. After his recuperation, he was reassigned to the Western Front, after two winter battles on the Eastern Front, he was sent to the Mediterranean near Marseille in France.

In later years he learned that most members of his former unit became casualties or POW's of the Russians.

The Germans expected allied landings in the future as part of the invasion to come. This turned out to be correct. For the next six months, stationed in France, he must have felt settled "in his trade," as he handled concrete instead of fighting battles. The beaches of Southern France were to be fortified. For this purpose, heavy concrete obstacles were to be planted below the waterline. My father was in charge of a group of French fisherman and their boats. The group moved out daily, weather permitting, placing the obstacles. The reader might think this was an unusual team alliance and wonder about the kind of a relationship that existed between the conqueror and the vanquished.

However, in the early 1950's my father thought seriously of vacationing in France to visit his former co-workers. That sure did not sound like a forced-labor relationship.

It was around that time (Fall 1943) that my father bought two dictionaries, one translated German to English and the other, German to Russian. Dad told his fellow soldiers, "We may need them at the end." He used the English version through his three weeks as a POW in the U.S. prison camp in central Germany. I used the very same book later to study English when I decided to emigrate. You might say it was a wise purchase in 1943 when Allied forces did land in southern France. As part of the invasion, the Germans retreated. Their resistance was not comparable with the resistance displayed at the Battle of Normandy and thus the Allied advanced quickly.

My father's unit task was now changed completely. It turned from a constructive to a destructive force, commanded to blow up bridges in order to slow the Allied advance. Their retreat took them through France and back into Germany toward the Russians.

In February 1945, Stalin requested that the Western Allies bomb Dresden in the state of Saxony. Dresden was an important railroad junction and supplied the Eastern Front; in short, a military target. I'm sure my readers heard about the air raids that killed an estimated 100,000 civilians owing to the unexpected fire storm. Strangely, two days after the attack, Dad rode on a German troop train through Dresden - the railroad yard was untouched, with no bomb hits. Another of war's mysteries.

On May 1, Dad and his fellow soldiers found themselves in a pocket surrounded by Russian, American and partisan forces. The German troops stacked up its weapons, ready to surrender, but when the partisans "offered" to take them, the German soldiers refused and picked up their arms again. Reason: the Germans decided not to play the waiting game any longer, but to turn west toward the advancing American forces. After meeting them, the Germans surrendered. Dad spent the next three weeks in an American POW camp before he was released and sent home.

He recalled two unpleasant things from his short captivity. The food was bad and there was little of it. There were just too many prisoners at one time, causing shortages. Before his release, an American Major delivered the "going home speech." In it he stated: "You will have many bad years ahead of you. We will not help you. Not that we cannot help you, but we do not wish to help you." Not exactly a cheerful sendoff, but under the circumstances, an understandable re-action.

The lean years lasted to 1948; then the Marshall Plan changed things for the better and gave the defeated nation hope again.

# Chapter 3

# Uncle Josef

Early in 1939 my Uncle Josef, my mother's oldest brother, who shared the milk delivery business with my mother, found himself disabled. It was the result of a bad back, as the ailment was called. He could not lift the heavy milk cans any more and sought medical attention. Medical science was not as advanced as it is today, but in spite of that, the capable doctors restored him to good health. They accomplished this with bed rest and the use of a custom fitted leather corset. It must have taken some time getting used to, but the result was that once again he could lift heavy loads. The treatment took place in a hospital in the city of Koeln in April 1939. Why do I remember that: It took place at the time of Adolf Hitler's 50th birthday, then being celebrated all across Germany. There were subtle signs of war preparations taking place and my uncle called them to my attention. A battery of FLAK (anti-aircraft cannons) was now stationed near the hospital, a questionable location.

After my uncle's hospital discharge, he continued in the milk delivery business until 1941.

The Eastern Front made heavy manpower demands. As a result, Uncle Josef was drafted into the army. The army was not about to spoil him with a soft job. After a training period, he joined an artillery unit in the east. He sent me a picture that showed him cradling a heavy shell. His unit had many Ukrainian volunteers who had joined the German cause to rid themselves of Stalin and Communism, but no such deliverance was in their cards.

Uncle kept a good relationship with his new friends, even learning to read and write their language. Later in the war, he and his comrades were sent to Normandy, France, an assignment that brought him into the Falaise sector, where the Allies launched an attack.

After many costly weeks of hedgerow fighting, General Omar Bradley found the solution. He applied massive air power attacks onto a small sector of the ring of German-occupied France. The

119

Allies succeeded in breaking the ring and advanced into the center of France.

Uncle Josef was lucky to survive the heavy bloodletting - he became of a prisoner of war. His next destination was a farm in England. Since he had always enjoyed gardening, he worked willingly as a farmhand. Again he learned the language of his surroundings. In the summer of 1945 he was discharged from England and returned home in good health.

# Chapter 4

# Uncle Hein

My mother's second oldest brother lived a few miles away from us. Since he worked in a plating plant, he was exempted from service until 1943. Afterward, drafted into the army, he served to the end of the war.

*Ludwig Wilhelm Knapp*

# Chapter 5

# Uncle Karl

Uncle Karl, the youngest of my mother's brothers, was by far
the most adventurous one. He was ten years older than I and
attended school in Dormagen, my hometown.

At the age of fourteen, he went to work for Bayer in the same
year that he was inducted into the Hitler Youth. Both the
training and indoctrination must have made a strong impression
on him because at the age of 17 he volunteered for the guard
regiment that was assigned to Adolf Hitler. Since his height was
6'4" and he was athletic and intelligent, he looked like a good
candidate. The requirements, however, were very demanding.
My uncle was rejected because he had flat feet, a physical
shortcoming that would keep him out of harm's way in the years
to come.

In the 1941 winter battle for Moscow, Hitler's and Stalin's
Guard Regiments faced each other. No prisoners were taken and
many idealists on both sides found a cold grave.

After my uncle received his rejection, he joined the German
Merchant Marine. His aim was to see the world, and he would
succeed in a way that he could not have imagined in 1937. His
first voyages took him to Spain and Africa. We at home received
his letters and sacks of native fruit. Since he was young and
husky, it was only natural that he would serve as a stoker, which
meant feeding coal into the boilers of the steam-driven ships. He
seemed to enjoy his new job.

In the summer of 1939 he came home on leave and told us that
his next trip would be to a far destination. The ship was the
"Sophie Rickmer's" with a capacity of ten thousand tons, then
bound for both China and Japan with artillery ammunition for
each country. Both Asian countries were at war at the time. Both
destination ports had German ordnance officers stationed at the
receiving points to serve as instructors.

When war erupted on September 1, 1939 the ship was in the
Indian Ocean near Sumatra, a Dutch colony. The captain decided

to try to reach a neutral port, rather than have to deal with the British Navy and risk capture.

The ship succeeded in reaching Sabang, a port located on the north shore of Sumatra. The next eight months, the ship's crew with little to do, were at leisure in the tropics and enjoyed complete freedom. They would learn about the progress of the war between Japan and China via radio news.

The peaceful routine aboard the "Sophie Rickmers" changed on May 10, 1940 when German forces invaded Holland. Thus, the captain gave orders to the crew, that happened to be on board the ship, to heave anchor and move toward deep water offshore. At that point the order was: "Open the sea water valves and get into the lifeboats." Since the Germans were now considered enemies, the ship would be seized by the Dutch - unless the crew's speedy action thwarted capture. But upon their return to port, the entire crew were taken prisoner by the Dutch authorities; their new address was now an internment camp. When the news of how promptly the crew sank their own ship reached Berlin, the entire crew was awarded the Iron Cross, 2nd Class, the medal awarded for bravery under enemy fire.

After the war, my Uncle Karl told me about the sinking with a big smile on his face. His own words: "I received the Iron Cross just like the rest of the crew, but I was watching a movie in town and did not go out to sea, as others did. I must have been the only German in history that ever earned this coveted medal while sitting in a movie house."

In 1941 when Japan came into the war, the tropical peace was again shattered. The Dutch on Sumatra turned the German prisoners over to the British. Their new POW camp would be in the Himalaya region of India. However, the British must have felt somewhat uneasy with this location in India, because their Indian subjects occasionally revolted. As a result, the ship's crew's next camp was in South Africa - again, not their final destination. In June 1943, the German crew found themselves on a transport to Canada, their last and final destination.

All this time, with little to do, my uncle had taught himself English. So at the age of 23, he found himself elected to be "spokesman" for his camp. Life at the camp was good. The prisoners kept themselves busy with all types of sports activities, and Uncle Karl participated in many of them. For productive work the prisoners dug peat moss. They also were allowed to write home and with the help of the Red Cross, were able to exchange letters. The crew must have enjoyed the peace and the beautiful land in Canada. When the war ended, many wanted to stay, but that was not to be. All prisoners had to return to Germany. Many, including my uncle, wanted to return, if possible.

In the summer of 1945, after an absence of six years, he returned to his hometown of Dormagen. He was lucky in comparison to his schoolmates, many of whom did not survive the war. He did not waste six years of his life fighting for an unjust cause. Besides being healthy and fit, he was now fluent in the English language. Since our hometown was occupied by British forces, he applied and was accepted as an interpreter.

Soccer, the popular sport in Germany, rose even further in favor after the war years. My uncle joined the local team, and soon he was one of its best players because of so many "practice years" as a prisoner abroad.

He worked as an automobile mechanic in the local shop. His aim was to return to Canada or travel to the USA. That all changed after he met and married one of my former schoolmates, Ursula Freese.

Karl was a good tennis player as well. He taught tennis to many people in our hometown, some who worked in management in the Bayer Plant. One of his students, the director of a department who held a Ph.D. in Chemistry, was so impressed by Karl that he offered him the job of a Shift Manager at Bayer. My uncle accepted this offer of a good-paying job since he now had a family to support.

By 1954 Ursula had given birth to their second boy and everything seemed to be going well, when Karl suffered a mild heart attack, from which he seemed to recover. He told me that years ago a nearby strike of lightning in Canada caused his heart problem.

He continued his job as shift manager at the plant until 1956 when he died in his sleep, the victim of another heart attack. At the age of thirty-six he left a wife and two young sons.

*Ludwig Wilhelm Knapp*

# Chapter 6

# Uncle Walter

My stepmother, who came from a large family, had seven brothers. Walter, the oldest of her brothers, volunteered to serve in the German Air Force. As navigator and bombardier with the rank of sergeant, he flew in the Western and Eastern campaigns as well as at the Battle of Britain. Shot down by the British, Uncle Walter found himself wounded and floating in the Channel off France. He was picked up by a German Rescue Plane. After he recuperated, he returned to active service on the Eastern Front.

Due to fuel shortages for flying, he finished the war not as an airman but as an infantryman on the Italian Front. His unit was designated as a paratroopers' company. It is a fact that toward the end of the war, the German command declared whole units to be either SS or paratroopers. The psychological advantage could not compensate for the poor training that these men would receive. Just one more irony of the war. He became a prisoner of war on the Italian Front.

Anyway, Uncle Walter's time had not come, and after captivity, he returned in good health to his family in Hanover, Westphalia.

During the last year of the war, due to heavy air attacks on German fuel plants, shortages became wide-spread.

I recall a joke on the subject. It went like this:

Did you hear about the new weapon? It is a forty-man — a two-man crew and thirty-eight men pushing the tank. . . . . . .

*Ludwig Wilhelm Knapp*

# Chapter 7

# Uncle Hugo

Uncle Hugo was younger than Uncle Walter and served in the Navy. He was a submariner assigned to missions along the American coast.

New crewmates on the submarine had to expect a "hazing," a form of initiation. Hugo told us about one hazing that ended in tragedy.

A new sailor was told to grease the torpedo tube. For this purpose the sailor had to don grease-coated leather clothing. Thus prepared, he would enter the tube and by crawling and turning himself around, would grease the walls of the tube. To scare the novitiate guy into thinking he was drowning, the torpedo tube would be closed and a little water would be sent inside. After a few minutes, the tube would be reopened and the hazing would be over. What a scary memory it must have left on the minds of many participants!

In this one case, however, too much water was allowed to enter the tube and the new sailor drowned.

The casualty rate of the German submariners, due to enemy action, was 80%, the highest of any service branch.

In his memoirs, Winston Churchill stated that he feared and respected German submarines. Uncle Hugo, one of the lucky ones to live to tell about it, returned home in good health after the war.

*Ludwig Wilhelm Knapp*

# Chapter 8

# Uncle Helmut

Uncle Helmut was another of my stepmother's younger brothers. He served in the infantry. Toward the end of the war, his unit was trapped by the Russians on an island in the Baltic Sea.

Since there was no way out, he and all his fellow soldiers agreed to surrender together. However, a group of their officers tried to escape by motorboat while the non-officers held off the enemy. This plan of abandonment aroused the anger of many of the rank-and-file. Thus, many of the officers became casualties from "not so friendly fire."

Helmut returned in good health from Russian captivity.

*Ludwig Wilhelm Knapp*

# Chapter 9

# Uncle Bruno

At the end of the war, Uncle Bruno, who also served in the infantry, was taken prisoner by the Russians. His POW camp was located near a coal mine in the Donets region of Russia.

To boost their production, the prisoners were divided into brigades of ten and were paid according to the brigade's output. They were told that the brigade showing the highest production would be released and returned home first. Bruno was a brigade leader and he devised the following plan:

All brigade members would pool their wages for the common good. The mining process involved first drilling holes, and then blasting in order to loosen the coal. The brigade's funds were used to buy extra dynamite from the storekeeper. (A little bribe went a long way.) These extra blasting powers enabled the POW's to moderate the depth of the blast holes and to avoid having to drill as deeply as was usually required. A guard checked the holes before giving the okay to blast and was only shown the very deep holes. Since these prisoners had a good relationship with the guards, they were alerted to expect a group of visitors on a certain date. The group consisted of high-ranking officers and party members who planned to inspect the efficiency of the mining operation.

Uncle Bruno and his coworkers decided on the following "stage play": When the visiting inspectors came into the mine, they were greeted with more than the usual drilling noise, because of the overpressure. That noise was followed by dead silence. When the inspectors asked about the interruption, they were told that something had broken, but that the POW's were repairing the problem. After a few minutes, pressure was restored, the noisy work resumed.

The next day the friendly guards informed the prisoner group that the visiting inspectors were very happy with their performance. As a result, soon thereafter, the Germans found themselves on their way home. It seems that the combination of collective work and a little "stage play" for the benefit of the inspectors won the brigade its early freedom. Bruno would proudly tell friends and relatives about his short career as a schemer and actor while in captivity in Russia.

# Chapter 10

# Cousin Franz Josef

My cousin, Franz Josef, whom an eager draft board doctor "volunteered" into the Waffen SS in 1944, told me the following story many years later:

He took infantry training - his unit was designated as a paratrooper company. The last time the Germans used paratroopers was in 1941 when they captured the Mediterranean Island of Crete, after suffering high casualties. One of the participating troopers was Max Schmeling, the former world heavyweight champion in boxing. When Max saw the hell he was expected to jump into, he grew very reluctant and balked at the plane's door. However, some bouncers soon "convinced" him. Although Max survived the combat that followed, the story of his behavior spread, illustrating that even a brave boxer was not eager to die for the Fuehrer.

Even Hitler was shocked to have lost so many of his young and enthusiastic troops - so much so that there were no more air drops of paratroopers. However, such casualties did not stop the Army from designating infantry units as paratroopers. This act was supposed to imbue those soldiers with the pride and spirit of the elite paratroopers, at least on paper. The reality was quite different according to my cousin.

His last fighting day started very early in the morning. The opposing enemy was the 1st Canadian Army in the Netherlands in March 1945. Under cover of darkness forty-two infantrymen and six tanks advanced toward the Canadian lines. When they were spotted, all hell broke loose. The enemy opened up with very heavy artillery fire that turned the whole horizon red. They clung to Mother Earth and had little hope for survival.

The infantrymen finally spotted a farmhouse after the artillery firing slowed down a bit. They made a dash for it and succeeded in getting into the basement. The basement was already partially filled with German soldiers seeking cover. Soon a radio message came from the German lines. It informed them that they were surrounded and should try to break out and return to their own lines. The order met little desire to comply. Lay low and wait seemed the wiser action. The Germans did not have long to wait. Soon a troop of Canadian Infantry reached the basement and gave the order to surrender, with which the Germans gladly complied.

When Franz Josef saw the actual number of tanks and artillery of the enemy, his thought was "Why did it take them that long to get here?"

After a few months as a POW in Holland, he was released and returned in good health to his parents in Neuss.

# Chapter 11

# My Good Friend, Adolf Krapp

In 1949, while I worked as an electrician at the Bayer plant in Dormagen, I met a former employee newly returning from one of Russia's POW camps. He was Adolf Krapp who had spent the last four years in the city of Kerch on the Black Sea. The Black Sea is known for its vacation resorts, but Adolf's camp did not fall into that category.

My friend had started work at fourteen years of age as an apprentice in Bayer's electrical shop. Besides being friendly and helpful to everybody and having a great sense of humor, Adolf had developed into a first class craftsman. Welding was one of his specialties.

In his early twenties he had joined the local soccer club and served as its goalie and was known for catching most eleven-meter shots.

Here is an account of Adolf in pre-World War II days: It was customary to decorate the plant at Christmastime. A decorated tree was placed on the floor of each department. Some grinch in authority must have disliked the idea. An order was issued: "No Christmas tree can be placed on the floor anymore." The tree on our shop's floor had to be removed.

The next day when the workers entered the shop, they found a decorated tree, suspended through the skylight, in midair. Adolf and a friend just did not like the idea of a Christmas celebration in the shop without a tree; so they found a way around the order.

In 1942 Adolf was drafted. Because of his skills, he was assigned to the Eastern Front to be a welder for a repair company of the army.

In March 1945, my friend Adolf happened to be on leave with his family. The war was coming closer to home as the American Forces approached our hometown. Adolf had to make a choice - to hide at home and eventually surrender to the Americans, or to return to his unit on the Eastern Front. He chose the latter. He served to the end of the war, when his unit surrendered to the American Army. They were turned over to the nearby Russians.

137

He was then sent to the port city of Kerch, on the Black Sea in Russia.

The Russian Navy has many of its homeports located around the shores of the Black Sea. Adolf served there as a mechanic and welder for four years in a Naval support shop.

Due to his congenial personality, he developed a good relationship with his Russian coworkers. He was able to make his own tools and frequently his coworkers would borrow them; despite official policy to the contrary, he always trusted them. Upon return of the borrowed tool, he always announced that the borrower had earned his trust. Consequently, he became very popular.

Many Russians in the shop told him secretly that they hoped for another war so that Stalin would get his ass beaten.

For welding work, good electrodes are essential, but they were not readily available in Adolph's shop. The shortage was met by the process of dipping steel wire in cement mixture; it worked.

It was a rule that no POW's could work on Navy ships. In Adolph's case however, the rules were bent whenever a difficult welding job was required.

My friend often received "invitations" to help. They went like this - A Russian shop supervisor came to him, placed his arm over his shoulder and said "Komm Adolf Hitler, Komm," thereby informing him that his expertise was needed for a welding job aboard a naval vessel. My friend then picked up his equipment, some of it which he had personally made, boarded the ship, and did the repair job. As a reward, he could join the Russian sailors aboard the ship at their chow line.

At another time he and another prisoner were told to feed the pigs. A bucket filled with kitchen scraps, etc. was given to them to take to the pigpen. Upon investigation of the contents of the bucket, they decided the pig feed was "not that bad" and proceeded to eat some of the bucket's contents. Bottom line: it was the first and only time that these POW's enjoyed a full belly.

After his discharge from Russian captivity, Adolf returned in good health to his wife and son. He was thirty-nine years old at that time.

He worked until the age of sixty, retired and reached his eighty-fourth birthday. I had the privilege of working with him for five years and valued him as a friend and role model. I kept in touch with him until his death.

## Chapter 12

## Another Alumnus of Hitler Youth

When I served my apprenticeship at the Bayer Plant in 1944, the shop walls displayed some tough work-inspiring slogans such as: "Hard as Krupp Steel," "Tough as Leather" and "Fast as a Greyhound." Those words were meant to produce a dedicated worker in the Hitler Youth Training Team as conceived by Adolf Hitler and his top men. Many of us, in our later lives, retained the emphasis on good working habits from our time in the Youth group, while rejecting the propaganda and the negative instruction.

Let me tell you about my friend, A.L. I visited him and his family recently. He had been my leader in the Naval H.J. in 1944 when taking the boat trip in Chapter 9. He came from an unusual family since his father had been a member of the Communist Party before Adolf Hitler's time. The Nazi propaganda convinced his father and other like-minded to give Hitler's party a chance to improve Germany...

The Brownshirts philosophy was: Treat the fathers decently and thereby gain a chance to train the young ones to your liking. A.L. is three years older than I. The three more years of Hitler Youth training, however, resulted in his "strong desire to distance himself from his father's Communist past", as he admitted to me. It resulted in his eager ambitiousness. He was promoted and worked to become a professional leader in the H. J.

By 1945 he found himself in the ranks of the German Army. A.L. was captured in April by U.S. forces along with many other thousands of German POW's at Remagen near the Rhine. There were too many prisoners at one time lacking food and shelter—and since their physical condition had already not been that good when captured, many of them died. A.L. and T.F., another hometown boy, did not want to be among the usual statistics and decided to escape. They succeeded and returned home.

After the war, A.L. finished his apprenticeship and transferred to Workshop K in another part of the Bayer Plant in Germany.

He was promoted and served in various capacities until his retirement in 1986.

He showed me his home which he shares with his wife. They both keep themselves in excellent shape by participating in various kinds of sports. His home and gardens can be classified as showpieces, achievements, just like his life - 110% in success.

A.L. told me about his homemade pesticide for his garden, a 24-hour soak of nettles in cold water. He has great results with it.

# Chapter 13

# The Story of a Former SS Man, Pushed into Success

During one of my return visits to Germany in the 90's, my friend, J.W. asked me to come along to participate in a game night. The place was a local pub within walking distance.

"Knobeln" is the German name for a guessing game played with matchsticks. It may be played by two to four players. The participant hides 0-3 wooden matches in his hand—then everyone takes a guess as to the correct amount of concealed matchsticks.

Several rounds are played until a loser is determined. He has the honor of paying for the next round of beer. This particular evening only J.W. and one other player showed up. After a few beers, my friend told E.F. (the other player), about my background and my life in the U.S.

It turned out that E.F. was about five years older than I and consequently was an active participant in World War II. He told me the following story about his war experiences:

"I wanted to become an officer in the armed service. The lack of higher education reduced my chances, and I entered the Waffen SS, which did not require the higher schooling. I volunteered as an officer's candidate into the Waffen SS. I had received some pre-military training as a member of the naval branch of the Hitler Youth in Dormagen.

"When I reported to school I wore civilian clothing, and this created some uncertainty as to how to greet others at the school. I met an NCO near the school and lifted my cap when greeting him. It was my bad luck that this was politically incorrect - besides, the unknown NCO was going to be my future drill sergeant! Upon my graduation he admitted to me that he never forgot the unmilitary greeting and made me suffer for it.

"I was assigned to a reconnaissance unit of the Waffen SS and as such we were used as a "fire brigade" on all fronts, east, west and south."

The reader may be familiar with the cruel side of the Waffen SS. Let me tell you about the more sensitive side of some of its members.

Our friend stated to us the following: "We were in action on the Italian Front. After weeks of combat, we were sent north of Rome for a few days of rest. It was a sunny day in 1944. We were cleaning our weapons when we noticed movements in a nearby group of bushes. One of our group went to investigate - he found an armed partisan observing us. He shot and killed the observer and returned to his group. On his return his fellow soldiers questioned him about his actions. They teased him and stated 'You should have brought him in, as a prisoner, instead of killing him.' The effect of this criticism - the SS man killed himself in front of his friends, not exactly a morale-boosting experience.

"Shortly after we were transferred back to the Eastern front. Enroute we stopped at a factory near the railroad tracks. The workers turned out to be prisoners from a nearby concentration camp. When listening to them, I recognized the Koelner dialect. I stepped closer to the fence and started to converse with a prisoner who happened to be a fellow Rhinelander. The next day that prisoner was found dead with a slashed throat. Probably done by a fellow prisoner for his talking on a friendly basis to an SS man. The SS might have had a similar rule against speaking to prisoners, but in this case it was the prisoner's code that was enforced. I swear that our combat unit never participated in, or knew of, any of the darker things the SS was accused of.

"April 1945 found our unit in Czechoslovakia. The final pocket was forming - many German troops were trapped. They waited to surrender to the Allies, but we still celebrated April 20th, "Unser Fuehrer's Geburtstag (birthday). We drank too much, nobody wanted to think of the near and the dark future. We surrendered to the units of the Russian Army on April 25, 1945, near Prague. There was no regular camp for us. We were kept in an open field and told that they may keep us for a future war against the U.S. Similar future plans were made by the American Army units for SS units that surrendered to them.

"But we had enough war and three of us had other plans. While we still had a chance, and the area was not "too secure", we attempted and succeeded in our escape. We traveled west, hiding and dodging. One day we spotted an elderly couple trying to move furniture from their home which was needed by the American Army. We decided to take a chance and help them to handle their furniture. This was a stroke of luck. The couple told us: Our son is also a member of the Waffen SS and you are welcome to some of his civilian clothing. We shed our uniforms for civvies. Their daughter had a room for us to rest and hide for a few days.

"Then the US occupation forces called all 'civilians' to register. We were told: The war is over. We continued on our way west and finally reached home.

"It was June 1945 and I was 20 years old and my name was on the American and German 'blacklist' because of my SS membership.

"I recall the day when an English officer accompanied by a few soldiers 'visited' me in our home. There was a picture of me in my Naval Hitler Youth uniform on the wall. The officer asked my grandmother about the picture and she replied: 'marine', the German word for Navy. The officer, not too familiar in the German language may have assumed I was a member in the German Marine Corps. As a result, the English visits to my home ceased.

"The harassment by the local German authorities continued however for a long time in the form of 'unwanted community service.' This continued for several months.

"Finally, my family attempted to stop it. We did the following - my father went to City Hall and asked when the community service invitations would stop. He was told that it would continue until your son becomes an apprentice. As a result, I stopped my business training and became an apprentice in a photo studio. I liked my new job, had talent for it, and succeeded in it."

Our friend, E.F. became the owner and operator of a successful photo studio, and he stated that he never regretted his change of occupation initiated by City Hall.

Bottom line: Do not fight City Hall.

By the end of the war, the Waffen SS consisted of less than fifty percent Germans. Due to the powerful German propaganda machine, Dr. Joseph Goebbels convinced many young men of almost every European country that they should join the fight against Communism. I understand that they even subverted ten members of the U.S. Air Force to join them.

*Ludwig Wilhelm Knapp*

## Chapter 14

## Only One Came Back

In the early 1930's my hometown of Dormagen had several butcher shops, all located along the main street. One of them was owned and successfully operated by Herr Dahl, who happened to be Jewish. Herr Dahl had served in the Kaiser's Army in World War 1 and had received the Iron Cross, 1st class, for bravery. He had a thriving business until 1936 when the anti-Jewish movement started. Business decreased somewhat, but he could still make a living. Many of his customers remained loyal to him, simply by continuing to use him as "their butcher" on a clandestine basis.

Herr Dahl had a son named Jacob who helped his father in the butchering business. His son liked sports and was a member of the local soccer team. The Dahls were a respected and well-liked family in town. For that reason, they did not feel threatened until it was too late. When war broke out, all Jews, including the Dahl family in Dormagen, were arrested and sent to various concentration camps.

Jacob Dahl was the only survivor of the Jewish community of Dormagen. His personality, youth, and health surely helped him to survive the Holocaust.

He still felt strong ties to his hometown and he not only returned, but convinced his future wife that they had a future in his town.

It was related to me many years later that in May 1945, on the day of his homecoming after the camps, one of his nearby neighbors seemed to have spotted a man who looked like Jacob Dahl. To be sure, he followed him. It was observed that indeed it was Jacob Dahl who proceeded to the home of Herr and Frau E., one of my close neighbors. Jacob wanted to know how his close friends, Peter E. and Jacob E. had come through the war. Frau E. told him that both of their sons had died as soldiers. Jacob was taken aback, but Frau E. asked him to stay and go through their sons' clothings to pick whatever he wanted since their sons had no need for the clothing any more. Apparently Jacob Dahl's clothing was badly worn and needed replacement.

He reopened his father's butcher store and successfully ran it with the assistance of his wife. Jacob again participated in his sport, by becoming a member of the local soccer team. Many remember him from his first games, how he played fiercely against the local British team, made up from Tommies of the local occupation forces.

Their daughter and husband still continue to operate the butcher shop in my town.

One more major reason that the locals got along well with the Jewish business people was the following: In many families - as the end of the month approached, the cash for groceries had run out. The non-Jewish stores were unwilling to extend credit in contrast to the Jewish merchants who extended credit willingly.

# Chapter 15

# Collaborators

In a discussion of any war where prisoners were taken, the subject of collaborating with the enemy and betraying fellow prisoners often arises. The German POW's in Russia were no exception. Russian authorities took advantage of the disunity of the time. When the war ended and the prisoners were sent back to Germany, the final event years later was not a happy one.

All prisoners, including the collaborators, boarded trains at the same time to go west. When the trains crossed the German border, or even before, the collaborators were seized and thrown into a river while the train was in motion. The guards looked the other way.

Russia, after the war, dealt very harshly with its collaborators and for that purpose built many labor camps in Siberia.

My information came late to me in 1947 as I recuperated from tuberculosis in Grossledern Hospital in the Rhineland section of West Germany. I would hear different POW's reminisce about their war experiences, often far from sympathetic with those they viewed as villains. Rather than transgressions, they viewed any counter-act as a potential threat to a fellow prisoner.

*Ludwig Wilhelm Knapp*

# Chapter 16

# Foreign Legion

In the summer of 1945, when many German prisoners were being held in POW camps, the French Army resorted to a new way of enlarging its Foreign Legion. Former members of the Waffen SS units were given the choice of working for years in a French mine - probably dying there - or of joining the ranks of the Foreign Legion, with no questions asked about their history.

As a result, France sent entire units of former SS units to Indochina. Many of them died for France, years before the U.S. became involved in Vietnam. The survivors received a pension from France for services rendered to its Foreign Legion and to the glory of France.

What a strange fate for a German soldier - to finish out his years for the glory of his conqueror. This experience is not hearsay. It was related to me by the relative of such a soldier, formerly a Waffen SS soldier. Far from critical, the relative voiced admiration that France kept its word to a former enemy and had even granted him a pension.

*Ludwig Wilhelm Knapp*

*Ludwig Wilhelm Knapp*

# Chapter 17

# Losses

It has been estimated that the total number of people killed during World War II is approximately fifty million. Germany's losses total seven million, for soldiers and civilians combined. This figure includes the missing.

Of course, all notices in Germany were preceded by the following words: "He died for Fuehrer, volk and fatherland."

In our family we received two missing-in-action notices. Uncle Gustav, missing in Russia since the summer of 1944. His unit was ambushed by partisans in a deep forest in the center section of the Eastern Front. He was married to Aunt Lina, my father's sister.

Kurt, one of my stepmother's brothers, was listed as missing. He served in the infantry with the Sixth Army in the Stalingrad Battle.

Many of our family's friends from the prewar years lost their lives, mostly in Russia. Two neighbors lost all their sons. At the beginning of the war, death announcements appeared in all newspapers. As the losses mounted, little news of them was printed less the mood of the people be demoralized; so, the announcements were usually conveyed privately.

As in all wars, sometimes the news of the missing was premature. My Uncle Joseph Paefgen fell into this category. First announced as "missing-in-action," he later wrote to his wife from a POW camp in England.

*Ludwig Wilhelm Knapp*

# Chapter 18

# The Reason for World War 1 and World War II

Never in history was a pistol fired with more deadly results than on the fateful day in Sarajevo, the nineteenth of June, 1914.

The immediate victims were the Austrian Crown Prince Ferdinand and his wife. It is true that a Serbian teenager pulled the trigger, but some questions persist forever.

The first attempt to kill the Crown Prince was made in the morning, but the bombs missed their target. Against advice, the Prince gave the Serbs another chance - he went through the city again in the afternoon. This time the bullets scored; both the Crown Prince and his wife were killed.

Today, it is quite obvious that the inbreeding of the European monarchies must have produced a few mentally inferior people. As a result three cousins, Eddie, Willie and Nikki, the monarchs of England, Germany and Russia got World War 1 going which in turn led to World War II - one generation later. As a result over sixty million people died. Yes, that was some pistol shot on June nineteenth, 1914!

*Ludwig Wilhelm Knapp*

# Chapter 19

# My Return Trip to the KLV Camp

When I was young, I spent over two years in the KLV camp in Lengefeld, located in the Ore Mountains of Germany. It was only natural that my thoughts returned to that site many times. Since some of my memories were not too pleasant, I endured "unpleasant dreams" for fifty years.

In 1980, when my wife and I attended a wedding party in Long Island, we met Karl Seifert. Karl was born in the Ore Mountains of Germany and he knew the town of Lengefeld.

Karl had worked as an aircraft maintenance mechanic for American Airlines for many years. He had suffered a stroke which left him unable to continue his job.

With his wife's assistance he had visited his home area in Germany. I offered to accompany them if they would take another trip. His advice was: "Do not go to Eastern Germany. Since you have a trade, they might not let you return and keep you there. I'm disabled so they can't use me and they surely liked to see me leave."

We were still in a "cold war" with the Eastern Block at the time. Needless to say, I heeded his advice.

This all changed with the "Fall of the Wall" and the reunification of Germany.

When returning to my home area, Dormagen, for a visit in 1991, I planned to see Lengefeld. Prior to our trip to Germany, I wrote to a friend, J.W. telling him of my hopes to visit Lengefeld. Since my friend, J.W., had also spent some time in a nearby camp during the war years, he gladly agreed to go with me. Our wives were reluctant to go and remained in Dormagen.

In a rental car, Jupp and I headed east. We had no idea about what we would find in the area that we had left nearly fifty years before, an area that had been under Soviet Russian Rule since 1945. It had been reunited with the West only one year previously.

After a three-hundred-mile trip, we arrived in Lengefeld without incident and reached the school that was my home for over two years. We asked for the caretaker of the school and were told he lived nearby. We found his apartment and met his wife, Frau Schubert. I explained to her the purpose of our visit and related our background. She remembered us as the "Dusseldorfer Jungens" (youngsters from Dusseldorf) quite well. Shortly afterwards we met her husband, Herr Schubert, a man of sixty-one years of age, who possessed an easy smile and an excellent memory. He took us through the same rooms where, from 1941-43, I had lived as a young boy while receiving daily doses of Adolf Hitler's philosophy. I became emotional when I remembered. The schoolrooms were in excellent shape, thanks to the tender loving care administered by Herr and Frau Schubert over the many years under East German administration. The rooms had changed little, except for the absence of the Swastika flags of a long time ago.

I asked Herr Schubert about the Lerchner family who had been caretakers of the same school in the 1940's. He told us that they had lost their position in 1945 at the end of the war because Herr Lerchner had been a member of the Nazi party. Hans, their son, aspired to be a teacher; he had succeeded and rose to the position of a principal in the East German school system. The son served in this position until the breakdown of the Berlin Wall which preceded a great many changes. At that point in time, history repeated itself and the young Hans Lerchner lost his prestigious job just as had his father in 1945.

At the time of our visit in 1991, it was quite obvious that with limited resources, Herr Schubert and his wife had done an excellent job in the preservation and maintenance of the school buildings entrusted to them in a difficult time.

At the end of that exciting day my friend, Jupp, and I looked for a bed and breakfast place to stay, and we were lucky in our choice. We found an attractive private home in Oberwiesenthal. The home was constructed of attractive brick and almost brand new. It was owned by Herr and Frau Kolle. We had lengthy chats with Mr. Kolle who had been a sailor on East German Merchant ships for many years. He told us about his life on board the ships that supplied Cuba and North Korea. With bitterness he told us that in both countries they were guarded by soldiers with rifles. This did not make them feel as the suppliers to a friendly nation as they thought they were, but more like criminals. He also expressed a great disappointment with their present leadership. He stated that many former Communists had simply changed their party labels without changing their convictions. He also expressed his concern over the damage done by acid rain and careless mining. Their son had left home and was working in the West as an apprentice.

Our room contained a guest register of the previous years. My friend remarked that it contained enough questions, for example, to fill a "wanted by Police" register, and I had to agree with him.

The next morning we found our breakfast ready in the hallway - the homeowners had left early for work and had asked us to lock the house and throw the key through the gap between the window and its frame. We felt sheepish since we were worried about the security of our rental car.

When we left, we both wondered out loud about how our hosts had managed to build a new home under difficult conditions. My friend concluded philosophically: Where there is a will, there is a way.

During our travels in Saxony, we were impressed by the amount of construction taking place, all done with West German Funding.

After ten years of West German aid, many people in the Western lands of Germany may feel little sympathy for their "Eastern Brothers," but all Germans feel proud of the bloodless reunification that was accomplished through the cooperative efforts of both Mr. Gorbachev of Russia and Mr. Kohl of Germany. Their nations showed the whole world what can be done, and many nations can learn from their example.

The bottom line after my 1991 trip to the East:

THAT WAS THE END OF MY FIFTY YEARS OF BAD DREAMS!

*Ludwig Wilhelm Knapp*

## Chapter 20

## The Berlin Maidens

During the years of occupation by American Forces in Germany many a G.I. married a German girl. It was no secret that a large number of soldiers enjoyed their stay in the country and developed a good relationship with its people.

In the early stages of occupation the "No Fraternization Rule" was in effect. From my own observation, I can earnestly state: It was largely ignored. To cover up, many a GI equipped their German girlfriend with a D.P. (Displaced Persons) armband. They were intended to be worn only by displaced person workers, who at that time were dispersed over the country, in war industries.

I've often thought about the reasons for so many frauleins becoming "warbrides." I settled on several: There was a shortage of young German males due to the large number killed in action on all fronts. Another reason: Maybe it was the trim figures of the young girls that attracted the eyes of the G.I.'s. Of course that figure was largely the result of many years of food rationing. During my last visit to Germany, a relative handed me a reprint of the first newspaper printed after the war in the city of Neuss in the Rhineland. The date is August 1945. The last page showed the Rhineland food ration for a week for a working adult. Notice, for example, that the adult is permitted no more than 2.5 ounces of butter, 40 ounces of potatoes, 10 ounces of milk. If you were able to stay healthy eating only this amount of food for several years, you had a very healthy body and good genes. Bottom line: You might make a good wife.

For any reader who might just be looking for an unusual diet, you may want to try it (at your own risk)...(See food ration list under Appendix.)

*Ludwig Wilhelm Knapp*

# Chapter 21

# Epilogue

In October 1954 I came to America at the age of 24, volunteered for service in the U.S. Army from 1955-57 and was trained for air conditioning service. While in service in 1956, I married Doris, who was born in New Jersey. We have two children, a son and a daughter, and five grandsons

Due to my trade training in Germany as well as in the U.S. Army, I was able to work at jobs that were both interesting and fun.

Besides my regular jobs, I was active for many years in the Boy Scouts of America, did maintenance work in churches and, for the last five years, have been working as a volunteer worker for Habitat for Humanity.

Although I lived, was educated, and was trained during Germany's darkest years, I have rejected the negative side of history and cherished the good coming from the country of my birth.

I have returned to my hometown for many visits, but every time I gladly return to the country of my choice, the United States of America. God bless it!

Ludwig Knapp

*Ludwig Wilhelm Knapp*

# Index

# About the Author

Ludwig Wilhelm Knapp was born in Dormagen, Germany in 1930, three years before Hitler's ascent to power in 1933. After his father was drafted and his mother committed suicide, his formal education landed him in a Hitler Jugend (Youth) School, geared to produce a model soldier. Before the collapse of the Nazi regime in 1945, he participated in trenching work for the Army along Gormany's western borders In the postwar period, he worked as an apprentice and later electrician for the Dormagen Bayer Plant. In 1954, he immigrated to the United States where his two uncles had lived since the 1920s. On arrival, he joined the U.S. Army, married Doris Gordon in 1956 and has since resided in New Jersey, not far from his two adult children and their families. During the twenty-eight years that he worked at Procter & Gamble, he served as a Scoutmaster for a local troop and more recently has devoted himself to Habitat for Humanity as a weekly volunteer. An avid reader of military history, he felt that it was time to record the story of the era he had witnessed first hand as a youth in Germany.

Printed in the United States
1549400005B/232-429